Dragon Scales

Dragon Speech Book 2

Margaret Ball

Galway Publishing

ISBN paperback: 978-1-947648-22-7
ISBN ebook: 978-1-947648-23-4

Printed in the United States of America
Cover art: Cedar Sanderson
Formatting: Polgarus Studio

Also by Margaret Ball:

Dragon Scales

1. Tectonic plates grinding

The trouble started on a perfectly normal Austin day in early March.

The bright, crisp morning with a hint of spring warmth had inspired me to wear a lightweight silky jacket over a silk camisole that just peeked out over the one button on the jacket. The light jacket looked professional but was the perfect weight to wear for my walk to the new office space on the Drag.

Halfway there, the sky went black with dragon-shaped clouds chasing each other from east to west and I was pelted with freezing rain. A superstitious person might have taken that as an omen, a warning; I took it as Texas weather.

Being superstitious would, in retrospect, have been smarter.

At first it worked out all right, because in the aftermath of the rainstorm a warm wind swept up from the south. By the time I ducked inside the front door of ShareASpace, the jacket was clammy but underneath it I felt too warm. I slipped into the as-yet-unlabeled door to our suite and peeled off the jacket, which was clinging damply to my skin. And my hair, which I'd tamed enough to tie back, was frizzing and trying to escape its Scrunchie. For the next few hours I would just have to work in a lightweight silk camisole over a skirt not quite wet enough to cling to my legs. What the heck – my business, my office, my rules, right?

My friend and tenant Laura is much more practical than I am about daily life, even if her professional life as a singer for alternative rock bands is the least practical career imaginable. Her office-warming present to me had been a box of office supplies, or what she thought we might need in the way of supplies. The anti-coagulant powder, the packs of gauze bandaging and the mini-fire extinguishers spoke to her opinion of me, rather than of offices in general. Fortunately, she'd also included such mundane items as markers, paper, and tape. I grabbed a sheet of paper, printed "Sienna Language Services" in big black capital letters, and taped it to the door. By the time clients were knocking at the door I would have something a little more impressive, but for today all I needed was something to help the people I was interviewing to find us.

I wasn't sure that I wanted to continue using a desk in the front room, but since we didn't have a receptionist I needed to be sitting there today to greet applicants and reassure them that Sienna Language Services was a real, if fledgling, business.

I hadn't exactly planned to interview prospective language tutors with nothing but thin straps covering my shoulders and nothing much covering the territory below that but some clinging apricot-colored silk, but it was a perfectly decent outfit. Technically speaking. I mean, my matching apricot lace bra was hardly visible, and anyway nobody could tell which bits were bra and which were camisole. As I sat down my business manager came out of the cubbyhole where he doubled as IT expert, and his eyes conveyed that the outfit was significantly better than "decent." From his perspective, anyway.

"I like what that color does for your skin and hair," Michael said. "Want to take an early lunch break back at the house?"

I had a feeling that what he really liked was the amount of skin exposed after I took my jacket off.

"It's nine-thirty. I have five interviews scheduled between now and noon, paperwork to file with the city before two-thirty, and more interviews beginning at three. Lunch is going to be a sandwich at my desk – if I can talk you into going around the corner and buying us sandwiches?"

"Ask and you shall receive," he said, "always providing I get the website debugged by then."

What? Yesterday he'd told me the website was functioning perfectly. He said he'd poked, prodded and misused it with every action from hitting the escape key to leaning an elbow on the keyboard, and all the screens came up on request and the information he entered got saved to the right place. Of course, that had been yesterday, and he had already been poking at the computer again when I poured my drenched self through the door...

"What have you been doing to my beautiful website?"

"Overnight I thought of a few little improvements," he admitted. "It's all your fault really."

"*My* fault?"

"I offered to bring pizza and beer over last night to celebrate our almost-opening. If you'd taken me up on that offer, I had some subsequent plans in mind that would have kept both of us much too busy to lie awake worrying about all the trivial details of starting a business. As it was, I can tell you didn't sleep any better than I did. Although," he added quickly, "those dark shadows around your eyes are very attractive."

"Liar. What's wrong with the website?"

"Nothing! I mean, nothing I did should have made the registration function crash."

"*The registration function crashed?*"

Lacking the gift of prophecy, at that point I thought that was the worst problem I could face today. If we couldn't sign people up for tutoring via the website, we would have no customers, hence no business. I could feel the blood draining from my face. I didn't have to check in a mirror to know that each and every one of the freckles spattered across my cheekbones and the bridge of my nose was popping out, accentuated by my pallor. Together with the raccoon eyes that Michael had so tactfully alluded to, my appearance alone would probably deter any prospective tutors from signing on.

"Well, sort of."

"Sort of crashed, or sort of didn't crash?"

"There's *no reason* for it to act up," he said impatiently. "Come over here." He popped back into the IT cubicle and I followed him. "Sit down, let me show you exactly what I did and maybe you can point out where I went wrong. See, I improved the font – picked a bigger, darker one – and that made the display window a little too small for the text, so I... Oh! *That's* the problem! Thank you, Sienna, you put your finger right on it!" He started tapping away at the keyboard and I went back to my own desk, wondering exactly how I'd helped him to solve his problem.

Against my better judgement, I flipped open my compact and looked at the damage. The rain had washed away my makeup and, just as I'd feared, the freckles were out in full force. I applied powder generously. "If I scare away all the applicants, we won't have tutors," I intoned. "If we don't have tutors, we can't help clients. If we can't help clients, we won't have a business."

It wasn't exactly a calming mantra.

Michael stuck his head out of the cubicle. "What are you worried about? Until we build up our clientele, you can handle them all personally."

"Only the ones who want tutoring in French, German, Spanish, Italian, Arabic, Russian, and Farsi."

"You left out Taklan." We'd spent a rather fraught time last fall in the High Pamirs, the mountains earlier explorers called the Roof of the World: not really enough time for me to have learned Taklan had it been a completely new language, but the two weeks we were there had been plenty long enough for me to pick up the Farsi dialect larded with Russian loan-words that was the national language of Taklanistan.

"Nobody wants to learn Taklan," I pointed out. "The university doesn't even offer a course in it. I might as well offer tutoring in the Language of the Dragon."

Michael shuddered. "Do you *mind* not calling it that? I'm trying to forget my encounter with the original native speaker. Anyway, you can't tutor anybody in that; you don't have the notes any more."

"True." In a sense. The original field notes to that dangerous language had been burned, rather spectacularly, by a gust of flame from that native speaker Michael was trying to expunge from his memory. He didn't know that I had pictures of every page in the notebook, discreetly stored on a thumb drive, just in case we ever really needed to explore the powers of that language again. And given his aversion to the whole subject, I felt he didn't really need to know this. I switched back to worrying about our ability to handle other clients. "Do you have that master list of all the language courses UT offers?"

"It's in your Documents folder. Do I need to show you again how to open it?"

"No." Meaning no, I didn't really need to look at the list again right this minute. *Not* meaning no, I didn't need help finding my way around the system Michael had assembled for filing, billing, scheduling, and the ten million records required by the City of Austin. I was just indulging in a bit of nervous fidgeting, wondering if we could possibly get everything covered before Monday's official launch.

You may have gathered that I'm pretty good at picking up languages. I'm also good at helping other people understand a language and how it likes to work. I actually enjoy getting them past that typical American approach of looking up each word of an English sentence in their little dictionary and then pasting the translated words together and expecting the result to make sense.

That was where Sienna Language Services was born. Blossom and Floss, my perennial Spanish-language students with a combined IQ significantly lower than the temperature of an Austin summer, had commented that it was a pity I couldn't bottle my tutoring approach and sell it to other tutors who didn't have nearly such good results.

And then Michael, who has completely unrealistic ideas of my abilities, had said, "Why not?" and the idea of my teaching a class for language tutors was born.

Somehow, over the winter, while for a change I actually worked hard at my day job of showing houses for my Aunt Georgia's real estate company, the initial one-class idea had expanded into the notion of a whole tutoring business, one where I would train tutors in my approach and oversee them as they did the bulk of the repetitive work involved in teaching a language to someone who was expecting to fail anyway. (People don't usually commit to paying a tutor until they're desperate, and by then they have a whole stack of bad habits to overcome.)

Somewhat to my surprise, putting actual effort into the real estate sideline had brought in enough commissions to start a small business on something slightly better than a shoestring. Aunt Georgia's take on the winter's results was that she always knew I had it in me to be a great realtor and that I must be crazy to want to drop the real estate business just when it was beginning to pay off for me. My take on it was that the winter's commissions were my running-away-from-home money. I'd never really taken to real estate, and now I had an honest-to-goodness alternative.

I had a registered business name.

An office.

A website.

Something faintly resembling a business plan.

And a chance to get started before the students struggling through spring semester language classes went down for the third time due to lack of good tutoring.

The academic calendar was pushing this start faster than I was comfortable with. As Michael kept saying, it would be silly to open a tutoring business in the summer when most of the university's students weren't even in town. As I kept saying, the beginning of fall semester would be a much more logical time to start the business, and that would give me another six months to get everything perfectly organized.

I don't know why Michael's logic overrode my logic here, but I suspect it has something to do with his personality and training. He's an ex-Special Forces type, loves challenges, and has total confidence in his ability to dominate any situation he's dropped into. That attitude seems to bleed over into his having total confidence in *my* ability to do the same.

Wish I felt that way about it.

After four interviews, one no-show, and an hour of working on forms intended to impress the City of Austin with our diverse staff and our commitment to historically underserved communities, I had a raging hunger headache and I needed to get out of the office. Forget sandwiches at the desk. I persuaded Michael to come out with me for an actual meal.

By the time we strolled back to the doors of ShareASpace, we were both feeling more human. We were even holding hands.

The sense of peace vanished abruptly when we were, oh, about one and a half steps inside the complex of shared offices.

"Mzzz Brown!" Rozzy Aguire, the ShareASpace manager, who'd been unfindable ever since I forked over the deposit, was suddenly a larger-than-life presence. She filled the hall between us and the door to Sienna Language

Services. "I really must insist that you remove *that person* immediately, before I call the police!"

Oh, hell. Was I late for the first afternoon interview? No, not yet. Had the interviewee shown up early and done something to spook Rozzy? Some of UT's foreign students did come from extremely strange cultures. Still, calling the cops seemed a bit of an overreaction to culture shock.

"What did he do? Or she," I tacked on, because I suddenly couldn't remember whether Sayana Raj, from Sri Lanka, was male or female.

"It's not what he did," Rozzy said ominously, "it's what he is."

I blinked. "Isn't that racist? What do you have against Sri Lankans?"

"Nothing," she said, "as long as they keep their clothes on! What kind of position are you hiring for, Mzzzz Brown? And that girl with him is obviously the kind of slut you'd expect to find clinging to a naked man. We have a strict policy against allowing ShareASpace offices to be used for *that* kind of business, Mzzzz Brown, and it won't take ten minutes to void your contract!"

I wished she wouldn't keep preceding my name with that "Mzzzz." The buzzing noise was beginning to vibrate unpleasantly in my head.

"Just a minute there," Michael spoke up. "Ms. Brown is not liable for *your* failure to prevent maniacs from invading your offices. But she might very well have a case against ShareASpace for letting this nut case into the space she is renting from you. Does the company have no concern for the safety of its tenants?"

He loomed over Rozzy in an intimidating fashion that was all the more admirable when you considered that he was only the same height as me – three inches shorter than the solidly built, six-foot office manager.

She loomed back.

Words were exchanged.

Menacing growls were exchanged.

"Guys, could you just cool it for long enough to let me find out what happened? *Both* of you cool it," I emphasized. Michael seemed to be reverting from his business manager persona to his previous life in Special Forces, and I didn't think guns and grenades were going to solve this problem.

Whatever it was.

I got my first clue after Rozzy grudgingly made room for me to pass down the hall to my own (rented) front door. I opened the door and saw two people: a pretty young girl who was familiar to me from a rather different context, and a very well-built man whose face did not ring any bells. It was, however, possible to fully appreciate how hot he was, because as Rozzy had hinted, he was stark naked.

His eyes gave me a clue: bright as gems, like glowing topazes, they were not quite human. I had seen those eyes before.

The language in which he greeted me was another clue. I'd heard that before, too. It was full of sounds like rocks breaking and tectonic plates grinding against one another. Both the people with me turned white.

In Rozzy's case I assumed that was because she didn't know what was making those noises.

In Michael's case I feared it was because he did know.

I filed for future reference that the being I'd met last fall in Taklanistan could change to a human shape at will. Although why he'd done so, and why that human shape was infesting my new office eight thousand miles from his home, remained to be explained. "*Chee khol doried*, Adjdaak?" I asked. "How are you?"

I was speaking Taklan, naturally. There was no way I was going to take the risk of brain damage that speaking the dragon's native language could inflict on a mere human.

2. Imagine Dragons

"You appear to be more intelligent than most humans," Adjdaak said, also in Taklan. Not that the switch from his language to Taklan made matters any more comprehensible for Michael and Rozzy, but at least Michael started recovering his color. Ever since Professor Osborne had driven himself mad by overusing the dragon's language, Michael had had a marked aversion to the grinding, grating sounds of that language. Not that he was in any danger of hurting himself that way; he couldn't pronounce a single word of the language comprehensibly. But I'd made some minor use of the language, frivolously using it to manipulate reality to my own advantage, before we figured out the price in potential brain damage that I was paying for doing so. And I think Michael was always just a little bit afraid that I'd succumb to the temptation to do it again.

Getting back to the current situation – compliments are, of course, always welcome, but they didn't answer any of the urgent questions on my mind. Like, what was Adjdaak doing here in America, when I'd left him hatching out a brood of dragon eggs in the High Pamirs? And why had no one ever told me that Adjdaak could shape shift? And – possibly most urgent – didn't he have anything to wear?

"That ignorant woman," Adjdaak continued, jerking his chin Taklan-style towards Rozzy, "appears incapable of recognizing my dragon nature in this form. And why is she so upset? Does she not appreciate my kindness in appearing in a shape that should be amply familiar to her?" He glared at me and I couldn't think why I had failed to recognize him at first sight. The dragon's golden eyes dominated his human face like two glowing topazes.

A lot of replies floated through my head and had to be ruthlessly suppressed as irrelevant, impolite, and unlikely to be helpful. For instance, the first thing that flashed into my mind was that I was not at all sure Rozzy was all that familiar with anything like Adjdaak's current form. She was certainly acting like somebody who had never been exposed to, ah, the totality of a man's shape.

Irrelevant. Impolite. Unhelpful.

"I too might have failed to recognize you," I told him, "had I not heard your speech. The Language of the Dragon is unmistakable!"

"Adjdaak, I *told* you this was not a good idea!"

Adjdaak's impressive aura was such that until now I hadn't thought much about the young girl who was with him.

She was a very pretty girl, with big brown eyes framed by a tumble of blond curls that fell unrestrained to her waist. Her clothes, while a definite improvement on Adjdaak's lack of same, might draw similar attention in America: a bright green flowered tunic falling to her knees, over baggy crimson pants pulled tight at the ankles, and pointed leather shoes laced up the top.

And in the long run, she might be even more trouble than her dragon companion. I'd met her during our excursion to Taklanistan the previous fall, and had made note on several occasions that I never, ever wanted to have a teenage daughter. Far too many things besides Rukshana's hairstyle qualified as "unrestrained" where she was concerned.

"Rukshana! What are you doing here?"

She jerked her chin up. Not pointing, this time; defiant. "I am running away from home. And so is he!"

Adjdaak growled something at her in his own language. His eyes glowed even brighter and small flames flickered around his nostrils and the corners of his lips.

Rozzy fainted, thus demonstrating that she hadn't been concentrating solely on Adjdaak's rather impressive dangly bits.

I looked at my watch. I had half an hour before the next interview; just time to solve the immediate problem. "Rukshana, Michael. *Don't let Adjdaak leave.*"

I was out the door before they had a chance to ask how the hell they were supposed to do that; on my way to Buffalo Exchange, where I picked out used jeans, a pair of large flipflops, and a T-shirt. By sheer luck – there certainly wasn't time to do any careful shopping – I found an extra-large black Imagine Dragons T-shirt with an artist's conception of a dragon pictured behind the Gothic lettering.

Adjdaak, as I might have predicted if I'd been bringing my full mind to bear on the problem, found fault with the picture of the dragon. Several faults. The hind leg joints were wrong, there shouldn't be scales on the wings, and the overall effect failed to convey the dazzling beauty of dragon form. He didn't stop complaining about it until I pulled it over his head and he was no longer able to see it.

I handed the rest of my cash to Rukshana and begged her to take him out for a walk up and down the Drag while I interviewed prospective tutors. "Buy him an ice cream cone at Amy's," I suggested. It was a pity I wouldn't be able to witness Adjdaak's and Rukshana's introduction to ice cream, but Amy's was notoriously crowded, especially on the first warm day of spring. Waiting in line for ice cream ought to keep the two of them out of trouble for quite a bit of what was left of the afternoon. "Bring him back at five o'clock."

Rukshana looked blank, so I took off my watch and put it on her wrist. "When the number on the far left is a 5 instead of a 2. And don't pretend you don't understand, I already know you learned to read and do arithmetic at the village school."

Only one more instruction. I fixed Adjdaak with my best you-*will*-memorize these-irregular-verbs look. "And Adjdaak, I also know that you can speak English. Please do so. You owe me for showing up unannounced."

Rukshana was inclined to complain that I had already failed in hospitality by forgetting to offer them bread and salt as soon as they arrived, but I didn't have time to debate Taklan versus American customs with her. As it was, they were barely out the door when Sayana Raj showed up for her interview.

"What are you going to do come five o'clock?" Michael asked between Sayana Raj and the next interviewee.

I probably looked wild-eyed; I certainly felt that way. "Take them home with me, I guess," I said while pulling out the pencils I'd stuck into my knotted-up hair whenever a bit of it made a break for freedom. "Find out what they're doing here. Find out if Rukshana's parents know where she is; they must be going crazy if she just took off without notice."

"I suppose that rules out a private celebration of the opening," he grumbled, and I reminded him that we weren't technically open yet.

***

I didn't actually get out of the office until six-thirty, and Michael was still antagonizing the computer system by speaking harsh words to it. I don't know what he ultimately did for dinner, but I decided to pick up a pizza on the way home. Two pizzas, after Rukshana tapped my arm and whispered that even in human form, dragons have a very large appetite. Three *large* pizzas, after she still looked worried.

I hadn't given adequate thought to the effect of pizza on palates used to, in one case, flame-seared sheep, and in the other case, boiled grain with not nearly enough salt. But I needn't have worried; after the first dubious bites, they tore into the pizzas with more enthusiasm than I'd witnessed since my one and only experience of overindulging in recreational drugs at a party in college. Adjdaak took care of two large Meat-Lovers pizzas all by himself, and Rukshana inhaled so much of the Veggie Sampler that I was lucky to get a couple of slices.

If I didn't persuade these guys to go home soon, they were going to bankrupt me.

After we ate, the next order of business was letting Rukshana's parents know that she was all right. I was dismayed, if not exactly surprised, to learn that she'd taken off without giving them a hint of her plans.

"They do not deserve to know," she said defiantly. "They hate me. They want to ruin my life. And they do not understand me!"

Her English vocabulary had certainly improved since last fall.

"If you knew how they treated me and Rustam—"

I held up a hand to stop the spate of complaint. I was probably going to hear far more than I liked about how nasty Rukshana's parents were to her boyfriend, but that wasn't an urgent issue. "Didn't you even leave a note?"

"Why? They are stupid ignorant peasants. They cannot read."

Briefly, I wondered whether Rukshana's parents even wanted her back. But that wasn't urgent either. Regardless of how she felt and how they felt, they had a right to know that she was all right.

Shaimak, Rukshana's home, was several hundred miles and a couple of centuries removed from instant access by telephone. I wound up spending far too long on the phone with the one American I'd gotten to know well in Taklanistan, an embassy employee named Jennifer McAusland. By the time I got hold of her it was four in the morning in Taklanistan and she was not thrilled about being awakened. Neither were the embassy personnel I'd had to pester to give me her cell phone number. Tough. I had a runaway teenager to deal with; I didn't have time to check time zones around the world.

I have to say this for Jennifer: once she was completely awake, she turned out to be exactly the right person to deal with the situation. I'd suspected as much from our encounter with her last fall. She was still involved with the young Russian colonel we'd met in Gundiz. (If you don't mind, I'll skip the explanation of why a member of the Russian army was in charge of a Taklan border fort; this book isn't about the geopolitical complications of Central Asia. Be honest, if it were you wouldn't be reading it, would you?) Jennifer's romance – this one; she seemed to juggle two or three such involvements simultaneously – meant that she knew a number of ways to get in contact with Gundiz.

"But I'd better go myself," she said, just as I'd expected once I knew she and Colonel Grisha were still an item. "If the pass is open, I'm sure Grisha will lend me a jeep to drive up to Shaimak. And if it's still snowed in, I bet he knows how to get hold of a helicopter."

I bet he did too. And based on past experience, he'd go with Jennifer, and the remaining space in the jeep or helicopter would be filled with bottles of vodka, and the Shaimakis would be happy to see him even before he told them what their runaway girl was up to.

What with one thing and another, it was nine o'clock before we were even ready to start on the explanations for how they'd wound up in my offices in Austin. And then, before Adjdaak even got started, Michael called with rather upsetting news.

3. Imperious and demanding

"What do you mean, you'll be out of town for a few days? What about the website? What about—" I couldn't even begin to list all the other things he'd promised to do. The biggest one, and the one I was ashamed to mention since it apparently meant so little to him, was that he'd be there to hold my hand after the website went live and I did what advertising I could afford and we waited for clients to show up.

"The website is fine," Michael said, "and so is everything else. I fixed the system again but you'd already left. And I just got you some free advertising: the *Austin Grackle* and the *Texican* both want interviews with you immediately, to run next week right after you go live. That's why I'm calling so late; it wasn't easy to set those up and make sure the timing is right. You're seeing the *Grackle* reporter at three tomorrow afternoon and the *Texican* representative at ten on Friday."

"I have people coming in for interviews!"

"Reschedule them. You seem to have forgotten that you're not asking the tutors to do you a favor. You're offering to increase their income at no risk to themselves."

"Except that our hourly rates may be lower than what they can get on their own, and they don't have to give anybody a cut of that. And if they insist on being paid cash, they don't have to pay taxes on it either."

"Made up for by the increased volume," Michael said airily, "not to mention your expert guidance and the offer of a supportive office environment."

Not everyone I'd interviewed so far had seen it quite that way. But he was right; most of them were eager to sign on.

"Also you're on live with K-TEX next Friday. The three o'clock show."

"I've never done live radio!"

"Well, you'll never be younger to start."

He must be feeling guilty about taking off like this to have arranged so much publicity so fast. And these were the perfect outlets: the Austin alternative paper, the university student paper, and the alternative rock station that most students preferred to the boringly respectable official university station. All I'd done, by contrast, was compose a flyer with phone numbers at the bottom that I hoped to persuade the language departments at the university, the community college, and two seminary schools to let me post. Pretty amateurish. Not only that, but I still hadn't finalized the flyer design. Every day I made some editorial changes and every other day I changed them back.

And I'd been counting on Michael to take the flyers round to the various departments, because he was much better at exuding confidence than I was.

"Don't panic," he said now, "with any luck I'll be back in time to hold your hand for the radio interview. Oh, and I've had some brilliant ideas for getting you on the local TV news as well."

'You,' he was saying, not 'us.' That only added to my feeling of being a sinking ship that the rat was fleeing.

"What ideas? Getting somebody stabbed in the office?" Our most prominent local TV station was a dedicated adherent of the 'If it bleeds, it leads' news philosophy.

He chuckled. "Nothing like that. But I'm not telling you now, because it'll just be one more thing for you to be nervous about. Look, I wouldn't leave if I didn't have to. But it's a job for Hank, and it's time-sensitive. And I do," he reminded me, "still have to earn a living."

Right. It was really selfish of me to expect him to devote every waking minute to being my unpaid business manager. He wasn't even living rent-free in the house I'd inherited from my parents – not yet – because by his quixotic standards he was still courting me, and you didn't crowd the girl you were courting by moving into her living space.

That probably went double when she was also the girl who'd greeted your first intrusion into the house with a Smith & Wesson .38 Special. Even for an ex-Special Forces guy who'd served in Africa and Afghanistan, that had been kind of upsetting.

Oh, we had a lot of history that could contribute to all sorts of misunderstandings and confusion. But I'd thought that we were past the misunderstanding stage by now.

Perhaps I'd been wrong about that.

I'd also counted on him to be beside me throughout this opening-a-business ordeal that had, after all, been his bright idea in the first place.

OK, maybe I'd been wrong about both things. I began to sag.

"They're announcing my flight now," he interrupted my private droop into the Slough of Despond."

"Wait! Where are you going? What are you doing?" I glanced at my watch. It was just after nine-thirty.

"You know I can't tell you any of that. Take care, Sienna. I'll be seeing you again as soon as I can."

He ended the call and I sank down on the couch, staring blindly at the litter of empty pizza boxes.

"It is too late to tell you of my adventures in coming here?" Adjdaak said. I thought he sounded hopeful, but his English intonations were odd.

Rukshana hit his arm and he winced. "Do *not* touch my forelimb," he warned.

"Oh, is it still weak and sensitive when you take this form?" she teased.

"*Nothing* about a dragon is weak. Or sensitive," Adjdaak huffed. He seemed to withdraw into himself, letting his eyelids droop until they almost obscured those amazing glowing eyes.

"I meant only, they were *my* adventures too," Rukshana said.

"Very well! Then I shall leave you to tell them. This language hurts my mouth. And it is intolerably imprecise." He folded his arms and sat back, sulking.

"First we—" Rukshana began.

"This country, this Merika, is much too large," Adjdaak interrupted her. "You see, it was—"

"So is this state of Taksus."

Rukshana flounced and folded her arms.

"Texas," I corrected absent-mindedly. "And maybe you're right, it's too late to get into the details tonight. Tomorrow, when we're all rested and refreshed, perhaps we can all be polite to each other and get a little farther." Besides, there was now something else I wanted to do tonight, and I didn't want to do it in front of these two.

But I *was* also dying of curiosity about them.

"Just one thing I'm wondering about." Trying to be tactful, I looked between my two sulky guests. "Rukshana, I know why you left home. But what about you, Adjdaak? Last time I saw you, you couldn't leave your nest because you were responsible for hatching the eggs your mate had left with you."

"And a very boring winter it was, too," Adjdaak responded. "But that task is over. The eggs have hatched."

"And the babies are already self-sufficient?"

Something very like a shudder passed over his body. "They are hatchlings. Imperious, demanding, and unwilling to acknowledge any limits."

Sounded like chips off the old block to me.

"Almost as bad," he went on, "as human adolescents." He glared at Rukshana.

"What does *that* mean?" she demanded, pushing out her lower lip. "What is an idle sense? I am a good worker!"

I intervened to explain that the word wasn't a pejorative. It just referred to her stage of life, between childhood and adulthood.

"Some girls not more old are married," Rukshana pouted, "and making babies already!"

"Perhaps your parents don't want you to assume that responsibility so soon." I said. "Babies are a terrible lot of work. Just ask Adjdaak."

The dragon-man shuddered again. "That they are. It is time for my mate to do her part. I sent for her before leaving. Now *she* can feed them morsels of fresh-roasted meat and teach them not to foul the nest." He looked distinctly smug at the conclusion of this statement, and lively flames flickered deep in his eyes.

Adjdaak might have been prepared to stay up and talk all night, but I was flagging. I needed some time alone to absorb the fact that I was on my own for the opening of this fledgling business Michael and I had thought up. Also, I needed to look something up.

It wasn't easy getting privacy. I didn't feel justified in putting up my visitors in the half of the house that my friend Laura rented, even if she was on tour with a band at the moment. I offered Adjdaak the front room which Michael had once rented, and suggested that Rukshana could share my bed for tonight.

I fixed her up with a spare nightgown, a comb, and one of the free toothbrushes the dentist handed out at every appointment, and thought I'd done pretty well by my surprise guest. I would figure out what Adjdaak needed in the way of personal grooming aids in the morning. For all I knew, he flossed with barbed wire.

I was ready to fall into bed and forget the world, but it wasn't that easy with Rukshana beside me. After an interminable period of bouncing and turning and twisting and kicking and sighing, Rukshana said that it was not possible to sleep on something so soft and bouncy that she might as well have been lying on Adjdaak's tummy. (In dragon form, I hoped.) She took both the quilts and made herself a pallet beside the bed and had just begun to snore when my cat stalked into the room. He had exercised his super-power of invisibility when I brought home strangers. Now he was using his other super-power to double his weight while waving his tail and complaining about the state of his food bowl. He stomped right over Rukshana to make his criticisms.

She bolted upright and screamed. I turned on the bedside lamp and explained that Cath Palug was not dangerous (as long as you didn't try to pick him up, get between him and his food bowl, or commit any other acts of lèse-chat). Rukshana must have been exhausted, because she was snoring again by the time I got back from filling Cath Palug's food bowl and clearing his litter box.

I was exhausted too, but there was still one more thing I wanted to check out. I pulled out my iPad and accessed the Bergstrom International Airport website.

There was exactly one flight that departed each weeknight at nine-thirty-five. A direct flight to Lincoln, Nebraska.

Nebraska?

Michael's patron, Hank Henderson, was a collector of exotic curios. What sort of exotica could you find in Lincoln, Nebraska? I did a little more searching. It was a university town and it had some museums, but I couldn't believe any of the conventional art and history museums would have acquired anything that Henderson would consider an exotic curio. Maybe one of the more offbeat collections? But I couldn't really picture Hank getting excited about something at the American Historical Society of Germans from Russia, or the Lester F. Larsen Tractor Test & Power Museum, or even the Museum of American Speed – always assuming that referred to race cars and not to meth, which I understood was wreaking considerable damage in the heartland. And none of the museums had been in the news lately with any startling new acquisitions or finds.

There was one thing to be said for Hank's hijacking of my boyfriend, though. When I finally did fall asleep, I didn't dream about disastrous business openings.

I dreamed that I'd missed a museum of American Dinosaurs, and that they'd just announced a major find in some wheat fields to the east of Lincoln.

4. A shallow ditch

On a cold March morning in Nebraska, Michael Ryan stared bleary-eyed at the ruler-straight road stretching out to a distant horizon. Periodically he took another swig from the cup of coffee he'd bought at a fast-food place in the outskirts of Lincoln. Well, it was probably coffee. Had been sold as that, anyway. From the taste he wondered if an addition of road tar had been what the proprietors meant when they advertised "Bold Dark Flavor!" Oh, well. It contained caffeine.

And it probably tasted worse because he was in a foul mood. He didn't *like* being pulled away from Sienna just when she was in a fine state of nerves about opening her business. And she ought to have understood that, instead of flipping out and practically accusing him of deserting her. What was he supposed to do when Hank Henderson, the man who actually paid him for work accomplished, needed him in a hurry? Did Sienna think he could live on love and air until such time as Sienna Language Services was making enough to pay a business manager? What was wrong with her, anyway?

He wanted to call up and put those points to her, more cogently than he'd done last night. But she wasn't a very nice person when awakened before dawn. Come to think of that, neither was he. Hence the foul mixture which the restaurant laughingly referred to as coffee, made barely drinkable by the half cup of skim milk he'd poured in to cool it and dilute the acid.

A pickup zoomed up behind him, apparently with obscene designs on the tail pipe of his rented car, then whipped around him and pulled in front so closely that he was surprised it didn't suck the paint off the hood. He got a good view of the double gun rack visible through the back window. Figured. Michael had no objection to rifles per se, but he preferred not to start a road fight with somebody who had two of them to his single handgun.

Not that it would be an issue... by the time his sluggish brain had made it that far, the pickup had dwindled to a dot on the horizon, and a mud-spattered sedan with a rusted-out passenger-side door was making the same quick dodge around him while leaning on the horn.

Local customs. Apparently regarding the posted speed limit as anything more than a polite suggestion was not one of them. Oh well, the car he'd rented had Nebraska plates too; he ought to get the same consideration from the highway patrol that these native drivers received. Michael pressed on the accelerator and discovered that his vehicle's maximum speed was a mere five miles above the limit. Anything more than 70 on this two-lane highway, and the car tried to shake itself to pieces. Anything less, and one of the large vehicles that kept passing him would come up on him so fast he'd be left as an ugly stain on the asphalt.

He sucked down the last of the "coffee" and kept his eyes peeled for the sign for Elville, Nebraska (pop. 650).

"Go 13.6 miles past Elville," Hank said he'd been told, "turn where Nelson's grocery used to be, then take the dirt track to the silos on the old Larsen place."

Not, Michael thought, exactly comprehensive directions – nor confidence-inspiring. Why would a legitimate seller want to meet at some building on an abandoned farm? Not that he should complain. If the deal had been entirely on the up-and-up, Hank would have met some respectable gentleman, probably at the Chamber of Commerce offices in Lincoln, and there wouldn't have been a job for Michael. Going into fishy setups like this was what Hank paid him for.

He'd meant to be respectful and observe local speed limits while passing through Elville, but the town was no more than a cluster of buildings around a single traffic light, and he was almost through the place before he slowed his pace enough to make a note of the mileage on the odometer. For the next thirteen miles he slowed to a decorous near-crawl and kept one eye on the odometer, one on the rear view mirror in case any more speed demon pickups attacked from behind him, and one – well, dammit, he *needed* three eyes even if he didn't have them. Okay, forget the speed demons and watch for a turn-off next to a building that might, some uncounted number of years ago, have been a country grocery store.

He got lucky, because the weathered building at the 13.2 mark had a sign that was still just barely legible as "N- LS- -S." And there was a graveled road beside the building, coming up at right angles to the highway. The seller must not have a very accurate odometer.

And he must be used to crappy roads, if he hadn't mentioned the quality of this one. The light gravel pinging off the undercarriage and sides of the sedan wasn't doing any good to this piece of Enterprise Car Rental's property. Oh well, Hank could afford to pay for minor damage to the paint job. It would be a drop in the bucket compared to what he'd told Michael he was willing to shell out for this thing if it turned out as advertised.

"How will I know it's authentic?" Michael had demanded when Hank called him the previous night. "You haven't even told me what you think it is."

The silence between their telephones crackled with tension. "I'm not saying anything on an open line," Hank finally answered, or rather, didn't answer his question. "But trust me, you'll know. You are *far* better qualified than I am to evaluate it."

"Why?" Michael all but howled. "Why me?" He needed the money but hated the unnecessary mystery. Why did Hank have to make his job so much harder than it had to be?

"Because of your travel history."

"Jesus, Hank, *you've* been all over the world. What could I possibly recognize that you wouldn't already know all about?" Before an early heart attack and subsequent health issues had reduced Henderson to being an armchair traveler, he'd traveled the globe from Bhutan to Belize, from the Seychelles to Samoa, in pursuit of the exotic curiosities he'd taken up collecting for amusement after he got bored with making billions in a variety of unromantic businesses.

A click and a buzzing tone were his only answer.

Now, as he crawled along this country road morosely counting the rattles and clangs as gravel hit the car, Michael wondered again what this mystery curio could be, if Hank had so much confidence in his ability to authenticate it. Okay, his military service had sent him first to some very unhealthy trouble spots in sub-Saharan Africa, and then to Afghanistan. None of the places he'd served had been part of Hank's globe-trotting history; even before the heart attack, Henderson had had too much regard for his health than to tour places where lead flew through the air and pieces of the roadside exploded on a regular basis. But Michael didn't feel he could claim much expertise in the kinds of things Hank was talking about. Sure, he could tell a Soviet AK-47 from a Chinese Type 56. And depending on what was left after the explosion, he could tell what had been a radio-controlled IED from one dependent on a tripwire.

But those were survival issues. He'd never had much attention to spare for cultural and artistic junk like the majority of Hank's collection. Oh, he'd heard the kind of words Hank used about his stuff, but they meant nothing to him and had nothing to do with his experiences in the service. A Congolese power sculpture was a painted chunk of wood to him. A Greco-Buddhist Gandharan relic in Afghanistan could as well have been one of the Greek statue reproductions sold by thousands around the Acropolis, except that the reproductions had less mileage on them and looked correspondingly better. If Hank was expecting him to make a connoisseur's appraisal of some obscure art piece that might or might not have originated in one of the hellholes where he'd served –

There it was: a group of three rusty silos, several hundred yards away from this road. And an overgrown dirt track with a double set of ruts angled off towards the silos. The battered pickup that had zipped past him on the highway was parked near the buildings.

And Michael had a very strong itch right between his shoulder blades. He *trusted* that itch. It had made him keep his weapon raised upon the approach of three adorable little Congolese boys who turned out to be child soldiers for the Lord's Resistance Army. It had kept him out of a house in Helmand

Province that went up to a Taliban-planted bomb seconds later. So… he continued driving.

It wasn't a hard call. He had a strong distaste for just driving up to a set of deserted, dilapidated buildings to meet some skanky type who probably had nothing even faintly resembling title to whatever it was he wanted to sell. He scanned the shallow curves of the landscape for something that might give him a little cover. A line of darker grass, leading cross-country from the farm buildings, caught his eye. The point where it intersected the road was some distance from the silos; all the better. He lifted his foot from the accelerator and the car drifted to a stop just opposite that green line. He eased himself out of the car on the far side of the silos and closed the door with infinite caution.

He peered around the car and decided that luck was with him here: as he'd hoped, the darker green signaled a ditch where the prairie grasses got enough more water to flourish. The good news was that it was easily deep enough to provide him cover as he worked his way back towards the meeting place. The bad news was that a ditch that deep and that green was almost certainly muddy.

There were worse things than a little mud. There'd been two rifles mounted on the rack in that pickup…

He edged around the car and verified that yes, the ditch was deep enough, and yes, the bottom was muddy. He still preferred it to the open ground. At least he could work his way up to the meeting place without being silhouetted against the sky.

Without having much chance to get away, though, if someone marked his slow progress by the movement of the weeds. A man could walk very quietly over the scanty grass; a man could stand over the ditch, weapon pointed, waiting for Michael to deliver himself within range.

Or, he told himself, a man could laugh his head off at the antics of the paranoid buyer who thought he had to sneak up on the silos as though he were approaching a terrorist fortified position. What reason did he have to anticipate violence? Yes, the rendezvous was a very isolated place, but that could be accounted for by a seller who didn't want anybody who knew him observing the meeting.

But the crawling feeling between Michael's shoulderblades, the sense that he needed to have his ears out on stalks listening for any anomalous sound – those couldn't be accounted for by anything but a gut feeling that had, more than once, saved his life. He would rather be muddy and ridiculous than ignore that sense of danger and rise to his feet.

Only trouble was, the ditch started getting shallower. Moving with infinite caution, he peeked through the weeds. Damn! The silos were still a good thirty feet away, and the ditch was going to run out within ten feet.

Slithering along until the shallowing ditch exposed him was not a good option. His sixth sense told him there were no good options now; he would just have to pick the least bad one.

Back up all the way to the car, drive back to Lincoln, and tell Hank that he'd been scared out of making the meeting by a creepy feeling between his shoulderblades?

He'd rather die.

Although, all other things being equal, he'd rather *not* die.

Gathering his feet under him, he sprang up out of the ditch and sprinted for the cover of the first silo. There was a muffled *thump* somewhere behind him, and a corresponding *ping* at the silo; he put on a turn of speed he hadn't attempted since Afghanistan and fetched up against the curved door of the rusty silo just as a second bullet smacked into the body of the silo at head height. The door wasn't latched; he dove inside and landed on somebody who grunted in surprise.

"Shouldn' a' come in here," a voice said.

"Why not?" Michael found his feet and estimated the other man's location from his voice. He was either a dwarf or was lounging against some kind of structure in the center of the silo. "It wasn't very healthy outside. Friends of yours?" He'd had the seconds necessary to translate those sounds now. A silenced rifle – which wasn't actually silent, but at least the suppressor muffled the obvious crack of a gunshot – and bullets hitting the silo, the second one closer to his head than he liked to remember.

"Not so much. They already got me. I'm gonna bleed out – good luck t' you, stranger." The slurring was worse.

Michael knelt, felt along the man's side, then his legs. He found a spot of spreading dampness on the outside of one calf. "No such luck, buddy. We're going to stop this bleeding, then we'll figure out how to get out of here." Good thing he'd worn a dress shirt for this meeting. Easier to tear than a T-shirt. And there were certain advantages to working for Hank; the man had arranged for Michael to get a handgun and his favorite tac knife through airport security. He felt on the ground around himself. Ah, excellent; a nice stick. He wouldn't have to use the hilt of the knife.

"Who you – callin' we – argh!" The wounded man's voice shot up an octave as Michael tightened the improvised tourniquet just below his knee.

"Oh, calm down. I've seen lots of people take worse shots and walk away."

"Yeah? Anybody ever tell you that TV stuff is all faked? And even if I could walk, they got a rifle. We got nothing. You think you're some kinda superhero, walk through bullets? You even have a plan?"

"One, stop the bleeding. Two, change the odds. Three, we have a little more than nothing."

Michael fished his phone out and looked at the discouraging screen. Zero bars. "You get any cell phone coverage around here?"

"Yeah, but not from a low spot inside a grain elevator."

That, at least, was fixable. But there wasn't enough light to plan his next steps. "Tell me what's inside this silo."

"Grain elevator, townie. In Nebraska, silos are where we keep missiles."

Great, the guy was feeling healthy enough to bicker. "Grain elevator," Michael conceded. "Any way to climb the inside?"

"Sure. North wall." Slyke elaborated until Michael felt he knew enough.

"Okay, now I need you to lie down."

A shaky laugh. "'Bout all I'm good for."

"On your stomach. Facing this way." He tugged the man over towards the rusted-out open spot at the bottom of the door and put his weapon in the stranger's hand. "If you hear movement, fire one shot – *one* – out through this hole. We don't have enough ammo to come out with guns blazing. But if they haven't rushed you yet, they're being careful. All I want you to do is encourage them to keep being careful until I get back."

The place between his shoulderblades itched as he got to his feet and moved over to the north wall. Trusting a total stranger with his weapon – was he crazy? Well, he'd find out soon enough.

"Hey! Where you going?" The man sounded panicked, not hostile.

"To improve our odds." He hoped the description of the north wall had been accurate.

5. The favor of his presence

While I scrambled a couple of dozen eggs, made skyscraper-high stacks of pancakes, and brewed three pots of coffee, Adjdaak and Rukshana finally told me how they'd gotten here… at least, in broad outline.

Adjdaak began by explaining that of course he had not flown all the way here. Being able to fly was one thing, he said. Being stupid enough to wear out your wings on a journey of thousands of miles was something quite different.

"Then how did you get here?"

"I used my Language, of course." Adjdaak looked mildly uncomfortable. "This Merika is *much* too large. The Language, as you may have observed, requires great specificity for successful use."

"You see, what he actually said was—"

"Hush, child!" Adjdaak interrupted Rukshana. "It could kill you to repeat my words."

"He only said that we were in Merika, I mean America," Rukshana pouted. "I think that put us in the center of the country."

"Oh? Where exactly?"

Adjdaak shrugged. "We did not remain long. It was not a bad place; there were sheep, and I was hungry after such a great use of the Language."

Something didn't compute here. "Didn't using it hurt you at all?" It wasn't just that I'd given myself migraines and slight memory problems from experimenting with the power of Adjdaak's language to reshape reality. Far worse had happened to Edward Osborne. He had used the scrap of dragon speech he'd just learned to change the weather around Shaimak, and using just that much power had turned him into a babbling idiot who subsequently walked off a cliff under the illusion that he could fly.

Of course, Dr. Osborne hadn't known that the words he spoke were going to improve the weather and save the harvest for that year. He thought he was invoking the Language's power to control and kill Michael and me, so I couldn't pretend to be totally shattered by the way he'd engineered his own demise. But it had made me very, very leery of using the Language myself. I would have thought Adjdaak, as a native speaker, would have been even more circumspect.

Now he looked down his nose at me, his topaz eyes glowing. "Of course it did not hurt me. It is *my* Language. You people have fragile and poorly organized minds compared to dragonkind, or you would not suffer from speaking words of power. This one would not even kill me a sheep!" he sneered at Rukshana.

"I *told* you it was not wise to kill that sheep," Rukshana interjected.

Adjdaak waved a large, dismissive hand. "It is not my fault that the people of this country have not been instructed in proper behavior. A single sheep is a small enough price to pay for the favor of my presence among them. Are you going to make more pancakes?"

Rukshana sighed. Long and loudly. While Adjdaak doused his second stack of pancakes in my roommate's authentic Vermont maple syrup and shoveled them into his mouth with one hand (I had decided that we could discuss forks later, when he wasn't so hungry), she explained that it hadn't been just one sheep. Stuffed with scorched mutton, Adjdaak had decided that they would sleep in a cluster of trees beside a nearby river. In the morning he would have another strengthening and reviving meal before renewing his search for Rukshana's American friends.

The only trouble was that his arrival and the subsequent sheep flambé-ing had not been exactly inconspicuous. Morning brought men with guns who had the impertinence to track Adjdaak from the remains of his dinner to the breakfast he and Rukshana were enjoying beside the river. Rukshana leapt on Adjdaak's back and begged him to leave immediately, but he could not believe that these humans would be so foolish and irreverent as to attack *him* – until the buckshot stung his flank.

"Tell me he didn't kill the people," I begged Rukshana while Adjdaak briefly stopped eating to express himself more fully on the matter of ignorance, folly, and irreverence among the peasants of America.

"That would have been excessive," Adjdaak pronounced. "Their little weapons could not do more than irritate me. I showed mercy."

"We just left," Rukshana corroborated his statement.

Neither Rukshana nor Adjdaak knew where they went next, except that it did not meet with their approval: flat, boring, no sheep and too many people running around screaming and pointing. Under stress, Rukshana remembered part of the name of the place where her American friends lived. Asking Adjdaak to convey them to Texas put them down on a highway with large green signs. Rukshana thought one of the signs read, "Brady," but she was not certain.

If I remembered my seventh-grade geography right, Brady would be near the geographical center of Texas. So Adjdaak's language took account of modern borders? Interesting. I wondered briefly whether they had first touched down in the geographical center of the continental United States. Where exactly would that be, someplace in Kansas? If it had been covered in my junior high geography class, I must have been daydreaming at the time.

They moved around for a couple of days; at one point Adjdaak scared a bunch of people out of a hamburger stand, where he and Rukshana made up for missed meals in a hurry of grabbing and gulping before the humans returned. When Rukshana remembered that both Thalia and I lived in Austin, she thought that they might ought to be a little more tactful in their approach this time. Also, she thought they must be quite close to Austin by now, so Adjdaak consented to approach the city by conventional means. Unfortunately, that ruled out night flight; I gathered that he had already discovered the dangers of things like radio towers and power lines. He had come gliding into the hills west of Austin just before sunset.

They didn't exactly manage to land unobserved, but from Rukshana's account, I suspected that the people lounging around the campfire where they first touched down had been *way* too stoned to say anything but, "Like, cool, man, a dragon!"

I hoped they hadn't been so stoned that they had the munchies, because Adjdaak helped himself to their sandwiches and beer before taking off again.

"How does he like beer?" I asked Rukshana.

"I do not like the metal," he said. "It hurts my stomach."

"Ah, you're not supposed to ingest the can."

"Those people were pressing the cans to their mouths. *My* mouth is big enough to take the whole can. Why would I not use the advantages of my dragon form?"

Oh, well. Not important. I wasn't entirely sure I wanted to teach Adjdaak how to chug a beer, anyway. Keeping him in pancakes and pizzas was going to be enough of a strain.

Not to mention coffee. Two pots had vanished down his throat before I got a cup for myself.

Now that they were within a few kilometers of Austin, Adjdaak said (between bites of his second serving of scrambled eggs) finding their American friends had been a trivial task for someone with his extensive and sophisticated array of nasal sensors. In brief – he'd sniffed us out.

Initially he'd been looking for my friend Thalia, whom he and Rukshana had known a lot better than they knew Michael and me; she and her husband had been stranded in Shaimak for several weeks after the terrorist incident a year and a half ago. But an unhelpful neighbor informed Rukshana that Thalia and Lensky and the baby were out of the country and she didn't know when they'd be back… so Adjdaak had turned his senses to locating Michael and me.

"The fact that the two of you are *erxtin* made it simpler still," he said.

"*Erxtin?*" I looked at Rukshana.

"Like me and Rustam," she said, and then scowled. "I mean, like we should be, only my stupid parents –"

"Later, Rukshana." I deduced that *erxtin* meant something along the lines of 'engaged, bonded, married.' "Um. Adjdaak, Michael and I are not exactly…"

"I know what you are," he said. "I can smell it: you are like my friend Thalia and her man. The bond smells rather like that between me and my mate, although of course it is not so strong – nor so beautiful. Still, considering what most humans smell like, an *erxtin* pair is an improvement on the usual."

Clearly there was some semantic space in the definition for more carnal interpretations. Except in that strictly carnal sense, Michael and I weren't exactly *erxtin* – consider his refusal to move in with me, for instance – but that wasn't an argument I wanted to have with Adjdaak. And I was quite relieved to learn that Rukshana and Rustam weren't *erxtin* yet, in any sense of the word. The last thing I needed to deal with was a *pregnant* runaway teenager.

Apparently our combined scent had left its strongest and most compelling layers around the new offices, because that was where it had led Adjdaak. I made a mental note that Michael and I had clearly been working too much and enjoying life too little. Something to be addressed on his return. If we had time.

Adjdaak was still annoyed about the amount of pointing and shrieking that had accompanied his stroll down the Drag with Rukshana and his entry into ShareASpace. He felt that he had been excessively deferential to local human mores by taking the form of a soft, weak human male to walk several blocks on a surface so hard that it would have been infinitely more comfortable to traverse it in dragon form.

"I don't think there is any form in which you would appear soft and weak," I told Adjdaak. "You should interpret these reactions to you as a sign of respect." There was also the clothing issue, but he was decently enough dressed this morning, so the details of American modesty taboos could wait for later.

Indeed, they would have to wait for later – I was barely going to make it into the office in time for my first scheduled interview of the day. And then I had to reschedule the afternoon interviews to give me time to meet with the *Grackle* reporter at three.

It would be nice to have some idea what I wanted to say to the reporter, but that might be asking too much of Fate. I felt that this would count as a successful day if I didn't stand anybody up and Adjdaak didn't incinerate anything. Or anyone.

It would count as a wildly successful day if I heard from Michael.

My next-door neighbor, Jenn, was watering the hanging flower baskets on her front porch when we left. There were trails of water dripping down from the baskets; clearly she had been determined to keep watering until she got a good look at my visitors. She called a greeting to me; I waved, smiled, and kept walking. Encounters with Jenn tended to last much longer than expected and to drain more information out of me than I liked. I didn't want to introduce Adjdaak and Rukshana to her at all, and I certainly didn't want to submit myself to interrogation until I'd figured out what my story about the unexpected visitors should be.

I'd intended to leave Rukshana in charge of Adjdaak while I dealt with the job interviews and the reporter. There was, after all, a very nice university campus right across the street from ShareASpace's offices. Red-tiled pseudo-Spanish architecture mingled with modernistic glass cubes; lots of trees; less fortunately, lots of grackles in the trees; green spaces between buildings, decorative fountains, the Turtle Pond. And lots and lots of other young people. Surely they could amuse themselves there for a few hours?

Evidently I'd been too optimistic. Adjdaak stamped back into the office, dragging Rukshana by the arm, just as I was saying goodbye to the rather shy young woman whom I had just hired to tutor Korean, Cantonese and Mandarin. Born in North Korea, she'd tried to get out and had been sold over the border to a Chinese farmer who wanted a wife, escaped him and made her way south to work in Hong Kong, got herself an education, and finally got herself accepted as a graduate student here in Austin. In other words, she'd already faced and overcome worse dangers and barriers than I'd ever dreamed of. So, if Kae Chiyong wanted to respond to personal questions by giggling and covering her mouth with her fingers before whispering a response, that was fine with me. Anybody who'd been through what she had should have no trouble keeping lazy or bewildered tutoring clients in line. Even when she whispered.

I wished Adjdaak would whisper; his new complaints were deafening.

6. The only genuine one in the country

Michael heard only two shots from the ground beneath him as he climbed the scaffolding, or whatever it was, going up the north wall. Good, his new "ally" understood the concept of conserving ammunition. He couldn't remember what this structure attached to the wall was called, but it didn't matter, did it? He didn't really care what the components of a grain elevator were called, he was just glad that some of them provided hand- and footholds to help him reach a better altitude.

At what he estimated to be one story above ground level his cell showed a tentative half bar that kept blinking on and off. Fortunately he hadn't run out of handholds yet. At two stories he got a solid two bars out of five; enough for his purposes.

His job done, he tucked the cell phone away again and descended somewhat less carefully than he'd climbed up. After all, he knew where the handholds were now – oops! Well, *most* of them anyway – and he would feel significantly happier when he was again the one holding the pistol.

"What'd you do up there, propose to your girl friend?" the wounded man crabbed when Michael made the last jump to the ground beside him. "Sounded like you were making a speech. What do we do now?"

He could, Michael thought, have shown a little appreciation for the fact that he'd been left with the only pistol. He could even have appreciated the fact that Michael had first treated his wound, then risked breaking a bone on the crazy structure of slats nailed to the north wall, and then returned. He could have ignored the wound, climbed high above eye level, and simply waited for this man to bleed out and for his attackers to satisfy themselves and go away.

Except that he couldn't. He'd never been able to be quite that cold, even in the middle of a war, much less in peacetime America.

"Made a few calls. Elville city police," he said, retrieving the pistol. "Elville county sheriff's office. Highway patrol… Now we wait for the nice men in the cars with lights and sirens."

"They'll scare them others away." It sounded more like a complaint than a wish.

"Yes, that was the idea."

"Aw, shit. Nothin' ever goes right for me."

"What, you'd rather have men with rifles shooting at you some more?" Rifles fitted with suppressors, which suggested the other guys had planned exactly this.

"I was gonna let you and them bid on it. Dammit! Why can't I ever catch a break?"

Because you're too stupid to breathe without reading the instructions? What had made this idiot think it was a good idea to invite two sets of total strangers to an isolated place where one set would walk away with the prize? To deliver himself and the prize, alone, to this deserted farm?

"Yeah, well, see, I wadn' ezackly s'posed to have it," the wounded man mumbled when Michael raised his questions in a slightly more polite form. "Old man Fletcher, he shot the thing. He figured it was his."

There was a very quiet crunching sound some distance away, as if somebody had stepped on some dead weeds. Michael fired through the hole in the bottom of the door and was rewarded by the sound of more crunching and retreating footsteps. "Who's old man Fletcher and what did he shoot?"

"*You* know. Adivarius Fletcher."

Well, somebody who gave directions in terms of 'where Nelson's grocery used to be' probably did think everybody in the world knew 'old man Fletcher.' "I'm his handyman, Slyke – Jason Slyke, that's me."

"What did he shoot?"

Slyke emitted a breathy giggle. "Won't ketch me that way! *I* di'nt see nothing! Could of been a bird… a real big bird. Eating a dead sheep, see? The thing took off right smart when old Fletcher used his shotgun. See, the thing that fell off where he shot it, he figured he had a right to it. But he di'nt know what t'do with it, did he? Me, Slyke, I'm smarter 'n they think. Took a picture, sent out some feelers. Your boss wanted it, so did those other fellers. *I'll* show you!" He struggled to get a hand into his hip pocket.

"Don't bother," Michael sighed, "it's too dark in here to see anything."

This time Slyke definitely giggled. "Dude. Doncha even know what your boss is buying?"

"He said I'd know it when I saw it. If it's the real thing."

"Oh, it's real all right." Slyke managed to jam two fingers into his hip pocket and pulled out the slender, flexible prize he'd been keeping under cover all this time. Michael drew in a long, shaky breath.

"Slyke," he said, "you are one hundred percent right. We don't need light, and it is the real thing." The subtle glow around the edges of the fan-shaped thing might have gone unnoticed in sunlight. Here it authenticated the object as no papers or provenance could ever do. And Hank had been right; he was the person best suited to recognize the thing. Not because of any of his military travel, but because of last fall in Taklanistan.

So that was what – or who — Fisher had shot! But evidently the shot hadn't been fatal. Not if the quarry had disappeared leaving only this fragment behind.

"Was there blood?" he demanded.

"*I'm* bleeding," Slyke whined.

"When your boss shot the – thing. You said it went away, and you picked this up afterwards. Was there blood on the ground?"

"Not that I saw," Slyke said, and Michael let out the breath he'd been holding.

"You going to pay me for it, or what?"

It seemed more than slightly absurd to bargain while they were crouched in an abandoned grain elevator, hoping the cops would show up before the unknown enemies out there moved in. "If we get out of this," Michael promised Slyke, "I will definitely pay you for it."

"How much?"

"How much do you think it's worth?"

Slyke giggled again. "A million bucks?"

"Are you out of your mind?"

"Not so much," Slyke said, "for the only genu-wine one in the whole country. How much does your boss want to own a dragon's scale?"

The wailing of sirens drowned out any possible reply. Which was fortunate, because Michael really didn't want to let Slyke hear the astronomical number Hank had mentioned to him. It hadn't been as high as a million, but not far off.

He heard brakes screeching, a car taking off, shots pinging off... something. Not the silo he didn't think. Then a megaphone blared, "Come out with your hands up."

"My friend's hurt," he called, opening the door a crack. "I have to help him." He hoisted Slyke up and got a shoulder under the man's armpit. "When we get out there," he told Slyke in an undertone, "give it to me."

"You got the money?"

Michael grinned. "My friend, you *want* me to have it. You're going to give it to me in full sight of however many police officers, and you'll just have to trust me to pay you a fair price. Because I don't think my competitors with the rifles just gave up and ran away. They'll be back – and before they get back, you want *everybody* to know that you just sold your thingamajig to the crazy collector from out of state. Don't you?

7. The god of lightning

"This girl," Adjdaak announced, glaring at me, "is rude, unmannered and completely unmanageable!"

"Uh-huh." Fifteen year old girl? From memories of my Aunt Milly's brood, most of whom I'd babysat while I lived with her in Beeville, I suspected teenage girls didn't come in any other flavor. "You brought her here," I said, "you take care of her."

"Impossible!" He shoved her into the room so hard that she bounced off Kae Chiyong. Who giggled, covered her whole face with her hand and peeped at Adjdaak through her fingers. I got the feeling she totally approved of him.

Not hard to understand. Adjdaak's human form made me think of those books that advertise themselves as paranormal romantic fantasy when a more honest description would have been paranormal porn. Maybe if he stayed in America he could get work modeling for dragon porn book covers.

Kae Chiyong's reaction to what looked like a handsome, six-foot, muscular male dripping with testosterone was perfectly understandable. It was also one complication too many for me. Great – not ten-thirty yet, and I was already in my personal red zone for crises. How much worse would it get before that *Grackle* interview at three o'clock?

By the time I got rid of Kae Chiyong, the room was filled with people. Damn! It was hard enough interviewing prospective tutors one at a time; I really didn't want to conduct group interviews. Had the people I'd cancelled for this afternoon been so eager that they decided to drop in this morning and take their chances at talking to me?

But that would only have accounted for two surplus people. Instead I had five – no, six – all talking at me at once. Well, two of them were talking at Rukshana, who was giggling and flipping her hair around. I glared at the other four. "Which one of you is Olatunji Ogunyeye?"

Not that I really needed to ask. It had to be the six-foot guy with the shining blue-black skin. Everybody else in the room was *way* too pale to be the Yoruba/Igbo tutor.

"That's me, ma'am," he said, stepping forward with a blinding grin. For a moment I was distracted by a brief fantasy of using him and human-form-Adjdaak as matching bookends. Didn't the English aristocracy use to hire matched pairs of tall, handsome footmen just to stand around and look impressive? I totally understood that custom now.

Olatunji's grin faded. "Ah, ma'am, I can also tutor Bini, Fon, and Ewe. And I know a little Hausa—"

Evidently he'd taken my moment of abstraction for some kind of disapproval. "No, no, Yoruba and Igbo are plenty," I assured him. "I've already got somebody for Hausa, and I don't think we'll get any clients for the other languages. UT doesn't offer courses in Bini, Fon, or Ewe." And I felt that I really didn't need to double-check Austin Community College's offerings. "But we do need to talk – if you would just wait a minute while I clear all these other people out?" I waved at a chair and waded into the remaining crowd.

"You, you, and you. What are you doing here?"

"Talking to *her*," one of the comparatively short, pale guys said, turning slightly away from Rukshana for a moment and then gazing into her eyes again.

"Well, you can't do that here. This is my office."

"Ok, we'll go back to the Drag." He took Rukshana's hand. "Is it true you never had ice cream before yesterday? I know this *fantastic* ice cream shop..."

Adjdaak said something in his native tongue. The combination of menacing, inhuman sounds and the flicker of flame around his nostrils totally distracted Rukshana's new acquisition from the matter of ice cream flavors. He even, briefly, appeared to lose interest in girls; at least, he turned even paler and started backing towards the door.

"Excellent! Adjdaak, could you do that again, please?"

A couple more flame-punctuated growls, and the two guys who'd been pushiest towards Rukshana had decided to find something else to do.

The ones who weren't going after Rukshana directly were a little smarter. "Isn't this the language tutoring place? I want to sign up for classes," one of them said.

"Me too," said a second.

"Give me a break, Billy," said the third, "you don't hardly speak *English*."

"Just cause you're bilingual don't make you smart, Manny," Billy retorted, "it just makes you stupid in two languages."

"What language do you want tutoring in?" I asked the one who'd spoken first, who just *might* be for real; Manny and Billy were obviously here just to elbow each other, whisper, and look at Rukshana.

"Uh, I don't know."

"Well, what language class are you taking?"

"Well. Um. None, actually, but I *might* take something next semester. And I already know I'll need a lot of help." His face brightened as something occurred to him. "What does *she* teach?"

"Nothing," I growled, "she's my receptionist, and you're interfering with her work. Get out – all of you!"

Adjdaak reinforced that polite suggestion in a manner that led to immediate compliance. But even after the room was cleared of people who had no business there, my problems were far from over.

Rukshana wanted to know if I'd been serious about having her work as my receptionist. It was a ridiculous idea – but her eyes were shining, and she no longer resembled the sulky, permanently angry teenager who'd been acting as if her entire life had been blighted by a conspiracy of us older folks. I couldn't afford a receptionist, of course. But then, I couldn't pay Rukshana, could I? She was the very definition of an undocumented alien. I was willing to give her ice cream money to get Adjdaak out of my way, but I drew the line at starting my new business by blatantly evading the law.

She didn't seem fazed by my explanation of why I couldn't pay her. I gathered that her aunt in Tireza and her parents in Shaimak and every other adult she'd ever encountered took the view that she owed them a full day's back-breaking labor, all day and every day, just for their generosity in giving her food and a place to sleep. Now I was providing the food and shelter, and I thought she might feel happier if she felt she was working for it. And I would certainly be happier if I had some kind of a leash on her until I could hand the responsibility back to her parents.

"Ok, you're hired. So to speak. We'll go over your duties at lunchtime, okay? I need to talk to Olatunji now."

I ceded the desk in the front room to Rukshana, with instructions to Adjdaak to back her up in evicting any more tourists who wandered in, and invited Olatunji back to the only other room with chairs, the little cubicle where Michael should have been working his IT magic instead of gallivanting around Nebraska for Hank Henderson. I made a mental note to ask Rozzy for more chairs; we needed two in each of the little rooms the tutors would be using.

Before we got down to the details of the job, Olatunji wanted to know about Adjdaak. Or rather, he wanted to tell me what he thought about Adjdaak. He shut the cubicle door, dropped his voice and solemnly warned me that he suspected the man in the other room might actually be Ṣàngó, the Yoruba deity of thunder and lightning. I should be very careful not to offend him, and it might be wise to wear red clothing so as to gain his favor.

I thanked him for his advice but said that I had known Adjdaak for a long time (well, it was beginning to feel long) and that I happened to know for a fact that he came from Central Asia, very far indeed from West Africa. Furthermore – though I didn't go into this trivial point – red was not a good color for me. There was a practically unworn red lace peasant blouse hanging in my closet that spoke volumes about my ability to deceive myself when looking at luscious outfits online.

Olatunji looked dubious and said that I should be particularly careful when the man spoke in that strange language of his, because everybody knew that Ṣàngó could call down his wrath and lightning on people by speaking the words of power.

41

Hmm. Words of power? Like the language of the dragon? Might be a good idea to look up this Şàngó when I had time. If that ever happened.

It was quite a relief when I could finally move on to the mundane details of exactly what I could offer Olatunji – a place on SLS's list of tutors, an office in which to meet clients, some guidance about how to teach foreign languages to Americans – and what I couldn't. I wanted all our tutors to be quite clear that I wasn't offering them jobs, merely the opportunity to do contract work for SLS if we had a need for their services. Michael had pointed out that not having employees would save me ninety percent of the hassle and expense of starting a business. Besides, "contractor" was a much more accurate description of the relationship. If somebody came to us wanting tutoring in Yoruba or Igbo, we'd call Olatunji; if they didn't, we wouldn't. Because his particular languages were so offbeat, I cautioned him that he shouldn't count on tutoring gigs as a significant part of his income. There might be whole semesters when nobody at all asked for help.

He grinned and said that from his observation of the Yoruba class, there would definitely be people needing help; the TA was an American whose grasp of Yoruba high, low and middle tones left something to be desired. Whether or not his students had the sense to ask for help outside the system… well, that was another question. He indicated that he wasn't signing up so much for the money as to enjoy social contact with people who were interested in his language and culture.

A tutor after my own heart, Olatunji. I made a mental note to put some notices about our services up close to wherever the Yoruba class met.

That gave me a brilliant idea which I explained to Rukshana and Adjdaak over lunch in the office. (Pizzas – enough for eight normal people or for two women and a dragon. Adjdaak was a disaster for my food budget.)

"I've been designing a flyer for our services which I was going to put up around town. Mostly at UT and ACC, wherever there are language classes." I brought up the latest iteration of the flyer on my laptop screen.

Rukshana looked blank.

Adjdaak picked up the laptop, turned it over, scowled at it, shook it, and handed it back to me.

Oh, right. That mostly snowbound village in the High Pamirs was not exactly a hot spot of twenty-first century technology.

Fortunately, the printer was working. I ran a quick check while it churned out a hardcopy of the flyer; the website was working too. The registration function was okay again.

I was in two minds on what to think about this. One way of looking at it was that Michael was a wonderful boyfriend who'd made sure to leave the system he designed in good working order before disappearing off to Nebraska to search for exotic tractor parts, or whatever the hell had piqued Hank Henderson's interest in the Cornhusker State.

Another view of the matter was that we hadn't had any computer problems since Michael left because he hadn't been there to fool with the system.

Hmm.

Maybe I should change the password while he was out of town?

Another thing to think about later. I grabbed my printout and skimmed it for typos before telling Rukshana and Adjdaak to wait there for me. It would have taken two-thirds of forever for my cheap printer to grind out a stack of flyers; fortunately, among ShareASpace's shared amenities was an efficient copy machine.

And maybe I shouldn't be too snide about my companions' difficulty with modern technology, because I had quite a time figuring out how to (a) enter the code that would bill these copies to Sienna Language Services and (b) tell the copier that I did not want mirror-imaging, collating, automatic binding, ice water, a manicure, or any other special services. I got it done, though, and Adjdaak was just polishing off the bones of the last pizza when I came back with a hundred copies of the flyer. Wildly optimistic? Oh, no. I had faith in Rukshana's ability to persuade anything male that he would love to have a copy of the flyer tattooed on his forehead, and certainly could not live without one attached to his classroom door.

"Ok, first thing, Rukshana, take the scissors and snip through all these little dotted lines at the bottom of the page. Like this, okay?" I demonstrated how I wanted her to turn a solid 8 ½ by 11 page into an 8 x 10 page with a bunch of separate little tear-off tabs that held my busnesss URL and phone number.

While she was working on that – thank goodness, at least scissors were familiar to her – I explained to Adjdaak what I wanted them to do. Rukshana's job was to persuade male department secretaries, language professors, and anybody in charge of a public bulletin board to let her post a flyer. As for the females, Adjdaak's first job was to work the same persuasion on them. His second job was to not let any of the nice people Rukshana persuaded follow her back to the office.

I printed out a list of the locations I wanted them to target – basically every place on either campus where language classes were taught – sent them off, and reclaimed my desk just in time to interview Vainamo Lindquist about tutoring Danish, Norwegian and Swedish. As a bonus, he was Finnish on his mother's side and was happy to let me add that to the list of subjects he could cover. I'd kind of hoped for that, actually, given his first name, but I hadn't been sure; his mother might just have been romantic about Finns.

After that, I actually had time to get a Diet Coke and comb my hair before the *Grackle* reporter showed up. And it was a good thing, too, because one of the subjects she wanted to explore took me completely by surprise.

8. The grackle woman

In the aftermath of the disaster, the three Russians huddled in an anonymous motel room miles away from Elville for an acrimonious discussion. "Zhenya, you are a blundering fool," Kostya began.

"Me, Kostya? Who's the idiot who thought it would be a good idea to start shooting?"

"What else were we going to do? We didn't have anything like the kind of money he was talking about. It should have been a quick, simple operation. He practically handed himself to us, with that meeting place out in the middle of nowhere. Show up, shoot him, take the *rakushka*, go home."

"Idiot. We can't go home until we find out where he got the *rakushka*. If there is a dragon in America—"

"I was going to question him before I killed him."

"Oh? So you didn't miss when you hit him in the leg? That was an exhibition of sharpshooting?"

Zhenya threw up his hands. "What do you want, Kostya? Kill him or not kill him? You can't complain both ways at once! Anyway, I did not miss, I just did not kill him with the first shot!"

"Giving him a chance to get under cover and for his armed friend to join him and for the damned *mentovoz* to show up. You're just lucky I had turned the pickup around so we had a chance to get out of there!"

"Yeah, you're always first to run away!"

"Zhenya. Kostya. Shut the fuck up. We have to figure out what to do next."

Nobody kept bickering when Bogdan said to shut up. An uneasy silence filled the cheap motel room. Eventually Bogdan signed. "Do I have to do *all* the thinking here? Zhenya, you're an idiot, but you speak the best English. You will go back to that village. They must have a tavern. Buy the local peasants some drinks, get them talking. We need to know where the other American was from."

"I can't take the pickup into the village," Zhenya sulked. "They will be looking for it. They have probably found the owner's body by now."

"Hitchhike," Bogdan suggested gently.

"Dangerous. It's all too dangerous. I'm not doing it."

"It is even more dangerous," Bogdan said, "to annoy *me.*"

Zhenya reconciled himself to the prospect of spending the next few years in an American prison. At least, if he got arrested and sent away, he wouldn't have to share a rented room with Kostya and Bogdan any more. This motel room was almost as small and depressing as his apartment back in Nizhny.

"Meanwhile," Bogdan said, "I will make contact with our masters and explain that we are going to follow the man who got the *rakushka*, only we will need more money."

"Why follow him? One scale from a dragon's hide is nothing. We cannot go home," Kostya argued, "unless we find the dragon. And if that was a true scale, then we know the dragon was in this part of the country, so we should continue looking around here."

Bogdan sighed. "*Bozhe moi*! My God, why do you afflict me with blundering fools? Kostya, the dragon *was* here, yes, but that was nearly a week ago. Have more sheep disappeared? Have the peasants seen more flames? The dragon is long gone. But this man who took the dragon's scale... how could he recognize it for what it was, unless he had seen the dragon? Find that American," Bogdan said flatly, "and we find the dragon."

"And then what? We have no..." Zhenya groped for the word. "No *budget.*"

"We have the tools we need, if only you deploy them properly." He gave the other two men a hard stare. "While Zhenya finds out where the American went," he said, "you, Kostya, will find a range and sight in the rifles properly.

46

When you two have a chance to shoot the dragon, I do not want you to miss. The Americans *must not* get a dragon." Especially when his own country had so far failed to acquire one.

***

I practically jumped out of my skin when the office door opened, but it wasn't the *Grackle* reporter. It was Michael, looking very tired and extremely pleased with himself. "What's got *you* all jittery?" he demanded before coming around to my side of the desk and kissing me.

"Mmm." I wrapped my arms around him. "I thought you were the reporter."

"What, you can't handle a little thing like an interview for the *Grackle*? What happened to the strong, competent woman I left in charge here?"

"Maybe it's a case of severe sexual deprivation."

"I haven't been gone *that* long!"

No? Sure seemed like it. I kissed him back. "It's complicated." I paused, trying to think how to explain the new problem, and we both spoke at once.

"You wouldn't believe—"

"You won't believe—"

We laughed. "Okay, you go first," I said. "What won't I believe?"

"What Hank wanted me to buy." He reached into the pocket of his windbreaker and drew out a bundle of fabric that looked like a hotel pillowcase. When he got it undone, he reached inside and drew out a thin, dark, fan-shaped thing that showed just the faintest flicker of light around the edges.

"One of Adjdaak's scales!"

"Unless there's some *other* dragon who's been rustling sheep along the Nebraska-Kansas border."

"No, that makes sense. When he brought Rukshana here, he wasn't very precise about his destination. I think the first place they appeared was the geographical center of the country. That would probably be some place in Kansas. Or Nebraska. Something like that… Why are you looking worried?"

"The scale. It was brighter yesterday."

47

"It's probably dying slowly. Not being a part of Adjdaak's body any more. Why, you think he won't want it back?"

"I hope not, actually. Hank would be disappointed."

"How much did it cost you?"

"Nothing, yet. Although in decency, I think Hank ought to pay the poor sap's hospital bills… It's kind of a complicated story. Your turn. What won't *I* believe?"

I had to think back. "Oh. Yes. Oh shit, she'll be here any minute! Thank God you're back."

"You're the head of the business," Michael said. "You're the *reason* for the business. You can't make me do the interview; it's got to be all about you."

"Oh. No, that's okay. I need you to do something else, actually. Go out to the Drag and make sure Adjdaak and Rukshana don't come in here until the reporter's long gone. I know, you can buy them ice cream. They like ice cream."

"Sienna, are you possibly just a tiny bit confused? This interview is going to be about you, your amazing talent for languages, and the godsend to confused language students that your business is going to be. It's got nothing to do with Adjdaak and Rukshana."

"Ha, that's what *you* think!"

To be fair, it's what I had thought too until the reporter called, just a few minutes ago, and I screwed up royally – although I tried to minimize that part when filling Michael in.

"She called around two-thirty and said she didn't want to cancel on me, but she was really busy chasing down another hot story and could I possibly just email her a press release?"

"I hope," Michael said, "you didn't let her get away with that?"

"Michael, I don't exactly have a lot of control over the lady. And you've got to admit, somebody starting a tutoring service in a university town isn't exactly the hottest news item ever mentioned. Especially for an alternative paper that specializes in covering the live music scene. But yes, she's coming."

"Why the long face?"

"I think she must be kind of new to the media business. She was really apologetic about canceling, told me something about this other story she's pursuing. Michael… it has to do with some people who saw a dragon in the Hill Country, a couple of nights back."

"Oh, no."

"Oh, yes."

"Tell me you didn't say that you had the inside story on dragon sightings."

"Of course not! But I may have… well…"

"What?"

"She asked why my voice went all squeaky. And then I may have stammered just a little. And she said that maybe she could find the time to talk to me after all, and she'd be here in twenty minutes. And I'd sent Rukshana and Adjdaak out to plaster flyers for the business all over campus, and I have no way to get in touch with them, and I've been terrified Adjdaak would walk back into the office while she was here and, I don't know, breathe fire at her or something. So you see why I'm so glad you're back!"

"What a disappointment. I thought you were overcome by lust for my body."

"Well, that too, but I don't have *time* to be lustful right now."

"When do we ever? If you'd mentioned this factor when you were trying to talk me out of helping you start a business…"

"It's not too late," I said. How had I ever let Michael sweep me off my feet in this way? Now my true, Austin-slacker, energy-efficient self returned to the fore. "We can take down the website, have Rukshana go back and remove the flyers…" I could have my old life back, the one where only stringent pressure from Aunt Georgia forced me into sporadic bouts of work that barely covered my groceries and the property taxes on the house. The one where I had infinite time to listen to my best friend singing with some of the best bands in Austin's live music scene, to watch old movies with Michael and miss the last third of the movie because we got slightly distracted, to work on my tan at Barton Springs when it got just a little bit warmer.

That had been a perfectly satisfactory life. But somehow, now it wasn't quite the seductive vision I'd anticipated. Probably I'd been working too hard and had lost some of my slacking-off skills. I hoped I'd get over it; being a workaholic would wreak havoc on my self-image as an Austin slacker, not to mention being no fun whatsoever. But just at the moment, I found myself strangely reluctant to abandon this mad tutoring enterprise just as we were about to get started. It *did* seem a shame to have put all this effort into it and quit now.

Which was just as well, because Michael wasn't about to let me back out. "I'll stand guard for Adjdaak," he agreed. "*You* will give this interview and talk about your gift for languages and your desire to serve the student body, and you will not allow the *Grackle* woman to sidetrack you into discussing dragons."

I snickered, and Michael gave me a dirty look. "What's so funny about that?"

"It's just – the way you said it. 'The Grackle Woman.' Now I'm picturing a bird lady."

He rolled his eyes. "Some days," he said darkly, "I can understand *exactly* why you hang out with those idiots Floss and Blossom."

"They pay me," I pointed out. At a conservative estimate, Floss and Blossom would require several hundred more hours of intensive tutoring if they were ever to pass the Spanish proficiency exams that would allow them to register as bilingual elementary education graduates. They were an even more reliable source of income than Aunt Georgia's real estate business. "Why wouldn't I hang out with them?"

"No reason," Michael said, "especially as you seem to operate on about the same intellectual level much of the time. Do you think you can stop snickering about feathered women long enough to impress the *Grackle* reporter with your language smarts?"

Doubtful, since I was long past being impressed by them myself. But it had evidently been a rhetorical question, since instead of waiting for an answer he took himself off to patrol the sidewalks in front of ShareASpace in case Adjdaak came back early. And a few minutes later I was seated across from Fern Monteith of the *Austin Grackle*.

She was a petite, fine-boned woman with feathery dark hair and a distinctly bird-like way of cocking her head on one side after she asked a question. No, I did not snicker. I merely observed.

"I couldn't help but notice, Sienna, that you reacted rather strongly when I mentioned the story about dragon sightings west of town."

Under the desk, I clenched my hands. My nails dug little half-moons of pain into the palms, reminding me to breathe slowly and act very, very normal. *Jeden, dva, tre.* Aunt Georgia had trained me to count to three before bursting out with what I really wanted to say, and doing it in Czech helped me to slow down. "Well, wouldn't anybody? It's such a crazy idea. I mean, *dragons*? Isn't that a little too much Lord of the Rings, even for the *Austin Grackle*?"

"Dragons aren't really a feature in *Lord of the Rings*," Fern said rather stiffly. "You must be thinking of Smaug in *The Hobbit*." Aha, an offended Tolkien worshipper. "And the people I'm going to talk to have pictures."

"Oh, sure they do. Which they'll be unable to show you when you get there! Honestly, don't you think they're just telling you whatever they think will get them your attention?" I sure hoped so. Rukshana and Adjdaak hadn't mentioned getting photographed by the people whose sandwiches and beer they'd stolen.

But would they have known they were on Candid Camera? Neither of them, as far as I knew, had ever been photographed before. It certainly wouldn't have occurred to them that the unimpressive little rectangular boxes in some people's hands were recording their visit for posterity. Dear Lord, I was lucky Adjdaak wasn't already starring in YouTube videos.

Fern smiled sweetly. "Oh, they didn't have to do that," she said. "This is the twenty-first century, you know. They've already emailed me some of the pictures. Want to see?" She handed me her phone.

9. Eyes like jewels

I had to stop digging my nails into my palms to take the phone. And just when I could have used the fingernail therapy, too. Oh, the pictures were not all that great. I'd seen more convincing images purporting to be UFO's, the Loch Ness Monster, or unspeakable alien horrors in Area 51. But to anybody who knew Adjdaak in his dragon form, the curve of the neck and the angular jut of the wings were quite unmistakable. *Uno, doi, tre.* People tend to forget that Romanian is a Romance language. I forced a smile, sighed quietly and handed Fern back her phone. "Afraid it just looks like a bunch of smoke and mirrors to me. Naturally I'll look forward to seeing what you make of it for the *Grackle*. But just for the moment, do you think we could forget about mythical monsters and talk about SLS's radical new approach to helping Americans with foreign languages?"

Ha! Just like that, dragons were off the menu and the interview was back on track. Why had I thought I couldn't deal with journalists?

Even being asked to explain, in twenty-five words or less, what was so special about this tutoring service couldn't faze me. After all, I'd been thinking about it for months; I'd written a page about it for the website, and then (after some bullying from Michael) had condensed that page to one hundred words; I'd written easily a dozen versions of what's-so-special for that flyer that Rukshana and Adjdaak were now – I hoped – posting all over campus.

"Americans aren't stupider than Europeans or Asians," I said briskly, "so why are most of us so hopeless with foreign languages? Lack of experience. If you spend your first eighteen years speaking only English, you're going to come to college with a *terrible* model of how languages work. You'll expect every language to act just like English only with different words."

"What's wrong with that?"

I gave Fern my friendliest grin. "If you went out looking for evidence to support the story you wanted to write, instead of trying to find out what actually happened so you could write the truth, you wouldn't be a very good – or successful — reporter, would you?" Granted, that comparison had only occurred to me because that was exactly what I thought she was doing with the "dragon sighting," but people tend not to recognize their own biases. Anyway, she smiled and nodded, and I went on.

"In the same way, someone learning a new language who expects it to work exactly the way the only language he knows works isn't going to be a very good – or successful – student. That's where Sienna Language Services comes in. We know enough linguistics to help students construct better mental models of the languages they want to learn, models that actually mirror the structure of the language instead of throwing away features you don't find in English or, worse, wasting time searching for features that English possesses but your target language doesn't. Do you know what the most common question asked in any American first-year language class is? 'Teacher, what's the word for 'the' in this language?'"

"And what's the answer?"

Could the woman be so clueless about languages? Oh, why not? She was a perfectly normal American.

"Usually," I said, "the 'answer' involves a teacher banging his head on the blackboard. Look – some languages have a whole collection of words where we have 'the', sorted by number and gender and syntactic role. Other languages have nothing at all. Tutors for Sienna Language Services understand that questions like that one represent a fatally flawed model, and they know how to help the student replace that model with one that actually works for the language they're learning. Until you get the underlying model right, there's no point at all in memorizing word lists or drilling on verb forms."

Fern's eyes appeared to be glazing over. Oops! I'd forgotten how that tended to happen when I started going on about how languages like to work. Not good. Boring the reporter into a coma wouldn't be good publicity at all. Even as I started panicking about how to retrieve the situation, she was standing up.

"It's all been very interesting," she said with about as much animation as a Non-Player Character in a video game, "but I'm afraid I must be going now. Articles to write, dragons to meet, you know how it is."

"I do." *And that's the literal truth.* Feeling rather guilty for having rambled on and on about languages, I tried to achieve an upbeat farewell. "Just don't look into their golden eyes. I hear that's dangerous."

"Golden?"

Damn! I'd forgotten the count-to-three rule. *Eins, zwei, drei.* "Well, ah, those pictures… maybe more topaz than gold, wouldn't you say? And definitely glowing. Like gems."

"You seem to have seen more in those pictures than I did. Maybe we should talk more…"

Oops again. Maybe I should take up counting to ten, except that would mean awkwardly long pauses. *Bir, iki, üç….* I seldom use Turkish, so remembering the numbers took a little longer than usual – long enough for me to come up with a response.

"Sure," I said as cheerfully as I could manage. "Tell you what, a concrete example is worth a ton of abstractions. How about we take a good look at consonant assimilation in Arabic and how that affects the forms for *al*, which is, of course, the Arabic for 'the'?"

She couldn't get out of there fast enough. My slip about the dragon eyes couldn't have been that bad; her aversion to Arabic consonant assimilation was clearly much stronger. Well, great. I couldn't charm or interest reporters, but at least I could get rid of them.

Michael was probably not going to consider that a great success. But then, I didn't have to tell him exactly how badly the interview had gone.

As it turned out, we didn't have time to talk privately until much later in the day. I had prospective tutors stacked up to talk with for the rest of the business day, and he found himself having to add a special early registration function to the computer system to accommodate the raft of people who suddenly wanted to sign up for tutoring before the business was even officially opened.

"I told you this was a good idea!" he gloated late that evening, over the open boxes of chicken masala and goat curry that littered the coffee table. "You're already swamped with clients, and we haven't even opened yet!"

"Mmm." I licked my fingers. One of the reasons we always got goat curry when we ordered out for Indian food was that I love the stuff but I refuse to eat it in public. Nobody raised by my aunts Milly and Georgia could bring herself to pick little goat bones out of her mouth in a restaurant.

The other reason goat was a regular feature of our orders from the Clay Pit was because Michael liked to compare it with the authentic stuff he'd eaten in Afghanistan.

It hadn't been quite such a hit with Adjdaak, whose idea of a decent meal was a couple of goats, not a few pieces of goat served up in a delicious sauce. And Rukshana was on the road to being totally Americanized; she'd whined about how she'd rather have a cheeseburger until I gave her a handful of cash and suggested that she get one cheeseburger for herself and a sack of them for Adjdaak. Now the kids were no longer whining and presumably replete; at least, they had stopped giving me grief.

"I'm not sure it's the business idea that's attracting these early sign-ups," I said, returning from the topic of goat curry to our *propres moutons*. "I think it's the Rukshana effect." The wave of attention had, after all, started just an hour and a half after I'd sent her out to post flyers. Adjdaak had, as instructed, seen to it that Rukshana didn't bring any of her dazed and persuaded victims home with her. But I hadn't told him not to give them our contact information; that would have been stupid, wouldn't it, seeing that we were doing the flyers precisely in order to spread that info?

I hadn't, at that time, quite realized that Rukshana's effect would extend to the guys who failed to get her phone number seizing on SLS as an alternative way to reach her. More than half the would-be clients who'd made my afternoon frantic had failed to fill out the part of Michael's *ad hoc* sign-up form specifying what language they were studying and at what level. Now I looked at the list of sign-ups I'd forwarded to my phone and shook my head.

"These kids aren't serious. They just want a way to reach Rukshana." I couldn't repress a very small sigh. "Being a dazzlingly beautiful young girl proves, once again, to be a better recipe for success than merely providing a useful service."

"You," said Michael, putting his arm around my shoulders, "are a glorious example of combining both features into one."

"Huh. I'm not dazzlingly beautiful. And at – well, closer to thirty than twenty – not all that young either."

"You dazzled me yesterday. What happened to that pink silky thing you were wearing?"

Yesterday felt like weeks ago, but after a bit of thought I decided he was trying to describe my apricot lace camisole. "I decided to dress more appropriately for the office today." Not that I'd exactly intended to be inappropriately dressed before; the soaking from a spring thunderstorm hadn't been in my plans either.

"A pity. I bet we'd have twice as many clients if you—"

"Michael Ryan, I'm not offering *that* kind of service!"

"What, not even in special private lessons?" He nuzzled my neck and tested the elasticity of my peasant blouse neckline. Turned out it was pretty loose. "Want to retire for a private lesson now? I'll put the trash out while you find that silky thing…"

I did want the clutter of curry leftovers and half-eaten naan out of my living room, so I didn't remind him until he came back indoors that we didn't at present have any private place to retire to. The living room had huge front windows that let in a lot of daylight but also made it practically a theater for anybody standing on the front porch. Worse, I'd never gotten around to making curtains from the blue and grey fabric that we'd bought to coordinate with the Ikea upholstery on the furniture. As for the rest of the house, Rukshana was sleeping on the floor of my bedroom, and I had given Adjdaak the room in front of that.

"We could borrow Laura's sitting-room," Michael suggested, and I was sorely tempted. My college friend Laura rented both bedrooms on the east side of the house from me. She used the back room as a bedroom and had turned the front room into a water-garden fantasy living room of Liberty cotton print cushions and flowing curtains. And she was away on a tour that wouldn't end for another few days…

A key grated in the front-door lock and I sat up and straightened my blouse. Had I misread the calendar? Because that certainly looked like my roomie stomping into the living room like a small black-haired tornado. She sniffed the air. "Curry from the Clay Pit," she announced, "and you didn't save any for me!"

"I forgot you were coming home today."

She gave me a black stare. "No, you didn't. I wasn't going to be back until Wednesday."

"What happened?"

"*Duke* happened," Laura snapped, throwing her carry-on in the general direction of her sitting-room door. "The pathetic idiot!"

"What did he do?"

"That man is too stupid to breathe without reading the instructions!"

Having enjoyed many a brief chat with Duke while he waited for Laura to finish doing her mascara, or whatever, I could find no fault with this assessment. I was, however, curious as to when exactly Laura had noticed Duke's mental condition. She'd seemed happy enough with his company up to now.

"It wasn't bad enough that he was *drinking* between sets." She toed off her ivory Louboutin stilettos and kicked them towards the door. I winced. I do not, myself, wear stiletto heels – I'm already quite tall enough, heels like those would make me three inches taller than Michael and neither of us would like that – and if I did, they wouldn't be $700 beauties from Nieman Marcus. But if I ever *did* happen to own a pair of shoes that cost as much as half of a round trip ticket to London, I would treat them with more respect.

"And getting drunk led to his taking another drunk's comments about the band personally." She threw her purse (Prada, not Louboutin, but ivory like the shoes and probably pricey enough to cover the rest of that round trip ticket) at the closed door.

"And as if that wasn't enough, he had to get into a fight and drag most of the rest of the band into it with him!" Laura collapsed into the chair on the other side of the coffee table.

"Ah… where exactly is Duke now?"

"He can rot in Hell for all I care!" Laura raked both hands through her artfully tousled black curls. They looked rather more tousled and less artful after this treatment. "Or," she descended to the mundane details, "in the Tarrant County jail, which is where I last saw him."

"What, they locked up the whole band? And why Tarrant County? I thought you were playing some place in Dallas."

"We picked up an extra gig at the Copper Coyote, outside Fort Worth. Kind of a dive, but good exposure." Laura completed the wreck of her hairstyle. "Or so I thought… but that, of course, was when I thought Duke had an IQ that was bigger than his shoe size. No, they didn't keep the whole band. Everybody else made bail. But *Duke*," she all but spat the word, "Duke, the genius, started a bar fight with his stash in his hip pocket."

"Pot?"

"Cocaine," she snarled, "and enough of it for them to make a plausible argument that he was dealing. He wasn't, of course. He just likes being generous with it."

"Ouch."

"You may well say ouch." Laura pulled up her legs to sit cross-legged so that she could massage her feet while she talked. Apparently even seven hundred bucks couldn't buy such a thing as stiletto heels that were actually comfortable to walk in. "And the sheriff of Tarrant County is running for re-election on a platform of zero tolerance for drugs. A long-haired musician from Austin with a Baggie full of white powder was like an early Christmas present for him. The tour's bust and I don't know if the band will ever get back together, not that I care."

She verbally dissected Duke's character, antecedents, and his probable bleak future for another half hour before she'd calmed down enough to pick up her ivory purse and heels and limp into her own rooms.

Michael and I looked at each other and shrugged. "We could go over to my place," he suggested.

I'd seen his studio apartment. It was not exactly a romantic setting, being decorated in Bachelor Minimal with a few mementos of war zones around the world, but it looked like the best offer I was going to get that night.

"The sheets are clean," he volunteered when I didn't shoot him down right away.

I was giving his suggestion serious consideration when Laura screamed.

10. The dragon in my back yard, part 1

She was standing in her bedroom at the back of the house, with her open suitcase on the bed, when Michael and I burst in and turned on the overhead light. She'd gotten as far as shedding the top half of her travel outfit before something outside the back window had surprised her into a scream and a terrified stare. Normally she wouldn't have been comfortable greeting Michael in nothing more than a skimpy black lace bra and her silky black trousers; now, it seemed, her state of partial undress was too trivial to worry about. I took a moment to drape her blue Japanese kimono over her shoulders while she was trying to get her breath.

"Laura, what happened? Somebody in the back yard?"

"N-not somebody. *Something.*" She clutched the kimono as though she were freezing, then slowly freed one hand to point. "Sienna, your back yard is… is… *moving!*"

The overhead light fixture made the room bright enough to apply makeup if you wanted to; the windows showed me nothing but glossy blackness. All the same, I peered. "I don't see anything, Laura."

"Turn the light off again!"

Michael flicked the switch and we all three peered at the night outside the windows. I felt my knees sag with relief. "Oh, that's just Adjdaak."

Laura gave me an unbelieving stare. "It's *sinister*, is what it is. I don't care what you call it. Sienna, what happened to the yard?"

All right. I suppose if you weren't accustomed to the company of dragons, the pattern of faintly glowing bluish fan shapes that undulated in the darkness might be rather startling. Both Michael and I had seen this particular light show before, in Taklanistan, but we had never talked about it to Laura. Well, if you were acquainted with a dragon who lived at the ends of the earth, *and* wanted your reputation for sanity to remain untarnished, would you talk about it to somebody who thought she knew that dragons didn't exist? Even if she did happen to be your best friend?

I stared out the window for a few minutes, trying to collect my thoughts. The undulating blue lines that edged Adjdaak's body scales were mesmerizing, as was the sweep of silvery wings and the golden glow of one open eye. In Taklanistan, in the daylight, he'd managed to make his dragon form seem like nothing more than a pile of jagged rocks. Here in Austin, for the first time, I appreciated the sheer savage beauty of that form.

Aesthetic considerations were probably not predominant for Laura right now. I began the long process of explanation.

"Laura, remember when I told you about this very strange language that somebody had brought out of Taklanistan?"

To be precise, they'd only brought out a field notebook full of transcriptions. Not a complete language by any means; just enough to give me an idea what the language had to be like. And later, enough to let me find out what I could do with that queer, rock-like, totally alien language – and how dangerous it could be.

Laura sat down on her bed with a thump that almost displaced the open suitcase. "Sienna, you told me you were never going to use that language again. And I'd almost managed to make myself forget about it," she said, sounding aggrieved. "*Now* what have you been up to? How did you change the back yard into *that* – and when are you going to change it back?"

"I didn't do a thing to the back yard," I said, beginning to feel somewhat aggrieved myself. I'd been polite and sympathetic when Laura stormed into the living room and interrupted Michael and me at a most inconvenient moment, hadn't I? I'd listened nicely while she spent all that time unburdening herself about that idiot Duke, hadn't I?

How come I still wound up on the defensive, when even a quintessential Southern lady like my Aunt Georgia would have had to agree that I'd exhibited flawless manners?

Another little thing to chalk up to Adjdaak's account.

"I never told you where that language came from," I said.

"Yes, you did. Katanistan – I mean, Tajikistan – I mean..."

"Taklanistan," I said, just to get the fumbling for syllables over with. "Yes, that's where the native speakers of the language reside. But you see, one of them recently decided to visit me here. I thought he was sleeping in the front room, but I guess he decided he'd be more comfortable outside; it's quite a change, you know. The girl who came with him insists on sleeping on my bedroom floor because she finds the mattress too soft..."

"Sienna," Michael said softly, "you're losing the plot. It doesn't matter where Adjdaak chooses to spend his evenings; Laura needs to know what he is."

"Ah. Right." I hadn't just been randomly rambling; I'd been putting off the need to tell Laura something she would think a sure sign of my descent into insanity. "Michael, you'll back me up on this, right?" I turned back to Laura. "The thing is... the native speakers of this language are not... exactly... human."

Laura's laugh was a bit shrill. "What next? They're space aliens out of Area 51?"

"Of course not," I snapped, "that's an urban myth. They're dragons!"

This time she didn't laugh. She just stared at me and started nibbling on her fingernails.

"Sienna's not crazy, Laura," Michael said gently. "Adjdaak really is a dragon. A shape-shifting dragon," he qualified. "Most of the time he's been here, he has been polite enough to assume human form. But I suppose he does find that a bit cramped. I'm guessing that's why he went out into the back yard and shifted back. Maybe if we turned on the back porch lights so you could see him better—"

"Not yet," I interrupted. "They're awfully bright."

"What, you're worried about hurting his eyes?"

"I just don't think it's a good idea to startle someone whose current form is as big as my entire house."

"Oh, he's only about half the size of your house."

"All the same."

I left Michael repeating his assurances to Laura in a carefully slow and soothing voice. I went out the back door to do the same with Adjdaak. I half suspected him of upsetting Laura on purpose – but then, he hadn't known that she was coming back, so he couldn't have planned this, could he? It was just that he seemed sulky and inclined to take offense. He groused that I should have known he would find the front room intolerably cramped. Foreign food was upsetting his digestion; why couldn't I simply get him a sheep or a couple of goats once a week? Why hadn't I brought him any vodka? And so forth and so on: bitch, moan, whine, complain. Anybody would think I'd been *forcing* American fast food on the ungrateful son of a... dragon.

Because my aunts Georgia and Milly had both put a lot of effort into seeing that my manners automatically defaulted to Southern-lady style, I did not point out to Adjdaak that he was an uninvited guest and that it would be perfectly fine with me if he were to go back to the Pamirs and find his own damned sheep. But it was a near thing.

"I think I know what the problem is," Thalia said when I telephoned her after she got back to town that weekend. Well, that was good. I'd only called to whine about the nuisance that was Adjdaak, but if she wanted to go into problem-solving mode I'd be only too happy to have the benefits of her experience with him.

"The problem is that he's a jerk?"

"Mmm. Different species, different expectations. He's rather like Mr. M.; I noticed that when we were in Taklanistan, the year before your excursion."

"Oh." I was not entirely comfortable talking about Thalia's friend Mr. M. We *had* been introduced; she said he was a great help in her work at the Center for Applied Topology. I couldn't see it, myself. By her account, he was a practically immortal turtle mage from ancient Babylon. Early in their acquaintance, he had had his head chopped off and his body destroyed by somebody who didn't understand him. "And you know, if you think he's unnerving now, whizzing around with his prosthetic snake body, it was *much worse* when he was a severed but undead turtle head," Thalia had told me.

It was her friends at the Center who'd located a robotics engineer who was talented enough to attach Mr. M.'s organic head to an inorganic snake body, and inexperienced enough not to realize that the project was impossible. Thalia got all vague when asked how they had made it work. She frequently got vague that way when the subject of goings-on at the Center for Applied Topology came up, and I'd learned not to press her. I had the general impression that what she called "applied topology" involved rather a lot of things I would be happier not knowing – just as Laura would probably have been happier not knowing that Adjdaak was a dragon. Well, too late for that now.

"Mr. M.," Thalia told me now, "gets just a mite testy whenever he's not the center of attention. Just like Adjdaak. Tell you what, why don't you let Adjdaak hang out with me for a few days? Brad's going to be out of town again at the beginning of the week, and I'd be glad of the company. Maybe he can sing lullabies to the baby."

"I don't think he sings," I said dubiously.

"Yes, well, most people wouldn't call what Mr. M. does *singing*, but he does it anyway. The baby doesn't seem to object, and at least Adjdaak has *hands*. Forelegs. Whatever. With Mr. M. to advise him, maybe the two of them could give me a break from doing Early Childhood Development twenty-four/seven. I mean, I love Aleksi to pieces and he is unquestionably the finest baby ever produced by an applied topologist, but I'm beginning to forget what it feels like to actually finish a – *no*, Aleksi, get that *out* of your *mouth!*"

Well, if Thalia didn't mind handing off the babysitting to a pair of supernatural reptiles with little or no common sense, who was I to object?

11. Tourism for dragons

The website went live on Monday morning, and for the entire day I was more than grateful to Thalia for taking Adjdaak off my hands. It was basically a very *good* surprise to discover that we were getting a steady stream of clients despite the handicap of starting in the middle of spring semester, but it was one neither I nor the website was quite prepared to handle. I'd been thinking of these first months as something of a test run, a chance to perfect the system without having to deal with too many actual students. Over spring and summer we'd work the kinks out of the system and I'd have time to train the tutors; then next fall we could hit the ground running.

"No battle plan survives first contact with the enemy," Michael said. He was being extremely calm about repeated website crashes as the registration function overloaded.

"I wouldn't describe our language students as the *enemy*, exactly." I pulled a coil of excessively lively hair out of my black Scrunchie and nibbled on the end of it while Michael tapped a keyboard and mysterious screens flashed by.

He gave me an amused look. "No? Don't teachers always think students are the enemy?"

"Not me!"

"Too bad you weren't teaching any of the courses the Army put me through. It would have been a nice change, having a teacher who wasn't trying to get me and everybody else killed. There, it was just an internal stack overflow. Should be okay now. I hadn't anticipated *quite* so much interest in our initial offering."

"Me neither." I bit down on the end of my wayward curl. "If I don't get all these people signed up with tutors and make sure the tutors use my system and get most of the clients past finals, we'll have years and years of no clients at all and plenty of time to fine-tune the system."

"I have faith in you," Michael said.

At least the scheduling function worked. By the end of the day I had fixed up a dozen tutors with one or more clients as well as filling my own schedule. Gabriela Gehrig had three beginning Hebrew students and she took it poorly when I told her that she'd have to meet with each one individually rather than lumping them together into a mini-class.

"I am only trying to help you, Sienna," she objected. "You are so young, you cannot be expected to understand the finer points of teaching. Three students together will work with and help one another. You poor girl, you really need an older and wiser woman's guidance."

It would probably have been counterproductive to say that I didn't see her as the person to provide said guidance. Instead, I told her that after the first three tutoring sessions, I would meet with the Hebrew students and explore the idea of combining sessions for a reduction in fees.

"No! It is not worth my time unless they pay full fees! Really, Sienna, I did not expect you to try to cheat me like this!"

"The clients are paying for one-on-one sessions. I can hardly ask them to settle for less without reducing their payments." Two more coils of hair burst free of the Scrunchie and writhed around my face. I grabbed a pencil, twisted them around the end and poked it into the gathered mass of my hair.

By the end of the day I had six pencils sticking out of my head, fifteen clients scheduled for tutoring sessions with other people, a full load of tutoring for myself, and a teenage receptionist in tears. *What* had I been thinking of, blithely planning to handle all the tutoring myself for the languages I spoke? Hadn't it occurred to me that since Russian, French and German were the principal languages that grad students had to demonstrate reading proficiency in, and since most departments held their language proficiency exams at the end of spring semester, we would be swamped by graduate students desperate to prove that they could understand the technical articles in journals like *Annales de l'Institut Fourier* and *Mathematische Zeitschrift*?

Well, no, it hadn't. Nor had it occurred to me that teaching people to read those articles might require just a little knowledge of the subject matter as well as fluency in the language. Thanks to Thalia's enthusiastic spreading of the word about SLS, a whole bunch of the graduate student clients came from the mathematics department. Maybe I could pay her to sit in on some of the more technical sessions, while Adjdaak or whoever watched the baby.

First, though, I took Rukshana home, fed her, and started the familiarization course I'd meant to give her first thing this morning. The bright-eyed confidence with which she'd begun the job had melted after a full day of trying to deal with technology she'd never encountered before. That was on me. In my world, a problem with my iPad or phone meant a consultation with my youngest cousin, who at fifteen was far more comfortable with the latest iteration of iOS than I was.

In Rukshana's world, iOS was incomprehensible magic. Well, to be fair, it was pretty much that to me too. It even felt like the actual magic of the dragon's language: I was pretty sure doing too much with it could cause irreversible brain damage. But like most people, I had my little collection of favorite apps. As long as I could open my contacts list, send and receive texts, read my Kindle books and play Angry Birds on my phone, I didn't worry too much about the underlying system.

Rukshana may even have had something of a head start on me, because growing up in a village with its own dragon had accustomed her to the idea of magic from childhood. It took me about an hour and a half to help her switch from doing magic by growling unpronounceable gnarly words to doing it by tapping bright little pictures on a screen. Then she took off on her own voyage of discovery.

"By tomorrow," she promised me, "I will know everything!"

Lack of self-confidence was never going to be her problem. I suggested that I would be quite happy if she knew enough to answer the phone, take messages, and direct potential clients to the website's registration page.

Then I got a text I had to deal with personally, so Rukshana would have to wait for the rest of her iPhone familiarization tour.

"No," I typed back to Thalia, "Adjdaak isn't here. I thought he was with you!"

"So did I."

Huh? Didn't she *know* who was with her? Texting was too slow; I speed-dialed Thalia. "So what's the story? And how could you not notice something the size of a dragon disappearing?"

"I wasn't here," she explained. "Ben wanted me to look at something in the office, so I told Mr. M. and Adjdaak to look after Aleksi. And I made it absolutely clear that they weren't to go anywhere with him! The trouble is, I forgot that Mom has the Flower Guild meeting at our church on Monday afternoons. Apparently she dropped by while I was out and took Aleksi to show him to the guild ladies. *Other* people's mothers," Thalia moaned, "live in the twenty-first century. *Other* people's mothers show their friends cute baby videos on their phones. Not my mother. She went off with Aleksi and left Adjdaak and Mr. M. at loose ends!"

She didn't sound panicked, so I leapt to a conclusion. "Your mom brought Aleksi back okay, right?" Personally, I thought Thalia didn't know when she was well off. *Some* people's mothers might freak out at the discovery that their precious grandson was being babysat by a dragon and a synthetic snake. Thalia had mentioned before that her mother had an impressive ability to ignore anything she didn't want to deal with...

"Oh, yes. He's fine. I was hoping maybe Adjdaak went back to your place."

I left Rukshana working on her cheeseburger and went back to check the yard. No dragon. Not even a vaguely dragon-shaped pile of rocks, which was his favorite disguise.

And he wasn't in the house, or he'd have followed the scent of cheeseburgers and demanded his share of dinner.

"Did you ask Mr. M.?"

"He says it was tiring to converse with Adjdaak in his language. When the dragon decided to go out, he took a nap."

Oh, Lord help us. What had Adjdaak taken it into his head to do now?

And could I find him before his wanderings around Austin triggered civil disorder, rioting, mass hysteria and a cult of dragon worship?

"I'm coming over," Thalia announced. "We need to put our heads together and figure out how to find him."

Sounded like a plan to me, except that my own head was coming up with absolutely nothing in the way of search techniques. "Okay." Since Adjdaak hadn't eaten with us, food was not an issue. "We've got plenty of cheeseburgers. Oh, and bring Mr. M. with you. Maybe he has some insights into the reptilian mind."

***

Adjdaak had quite enjoyed his reunion with Thalia Lensky, but once she left him and Mr. M. with the baby he began to feel bored. He had, after all, just traveled halfway around the world to get away from his own hatchlings. He did not particularly wish to spend more time with this little human hatchling, especially as he suspected the child was retarded.

"There is nothing wrong with Aleksi," Mr. M. corrected his assessment with a sniff. "Clearly you are unfamiliar with the milestones of human development."

Adjdaak pointed out that he had been living on the outskirts of a whole village full of humans for the hundred years since his birth in the great earthquake.

"Much too young for responsibility!" Mr. M. sniffed again. "And how many human hatchlings have you cared for in that short span of time?"

Well, none, actually. Why should he? He'd always thought they were boring, and this one here only reinforced his views. And no matter how much Mr. M. expatiated on the amazing cleverness of this hatchling in waving its arms, making incomprehensible speeches, and scooting across the carpet to grab anything hot or sharp or dangerous in the room, Adjdaak was still bored. He was more than happy to let Thalia's mother take the squirming little larval form.

Mr. M. might just possibly have found it more tiring than he admitted, chasing the little squirmer around to prevent it from killing itself. Once they were alone, he mentioned that his hibernation that winter had been broken up by far too much stuff to do with human babies, and announced his intention of taking a refreshing nap now that they had the chance.

Adjdaak did not feel in need of a refreshing nap. He felt more interested in adventure. Sightseeing. And, possibly, in obtaining some of that delicious clear liquid like the stuff that the Russian colonel always brought with him on his visits to Shaimak village. He would have asked Mr. M. where to find vodka, if the capricious turtle-snake hadn't already been snoring. As it was, he would just have to rely on his dragon ingenuity and sense of smell.

The flight back to Sienna's house was trivial, no more than a refreshing stretch of his wings. It wasn't worth the effort of flying at high altitude. But he did find the screams and pointing from the ground-bound mammals to be rather annoying. He decided to shift into human form for his vodka search. Being mobbed by worshippers could ruin a nice quiet drinking hour.

He made the shift in the back yard and strolled into the house after saying, "*Q!lv djmoq.*" The locks on the back door popped out of the door and rattled on the concrete steps. This place seemed excessively vulnerable to the Language; he'd meant to open the locks, not to destroy them.

The day had turned chilly; nothing noticeable in his dragon form, but the cold breezes raised goose-pimples on the naked flesh of his human body. Oh, right, Sienna had made a big fuss about the concept of covering up the human form at all times, unless he wanted to elicit more screams and pointing. Adjdaak sighed. Anything for a quiet life… He sniffed the still air inside the house but did not recognize the distinctive scent of his jeans and shirt, even though he had worn them for several days and the clothing should have been imbued with his dragon scent. No problem. Rukshana had already commented with some envy on the contents of their hostess's closets; Sienna kept a supply of garments that would have been the envy of the richest headman in the greenest valley of the Pamirs. It would have been a gross failure of hospitality to begrudge a few of them to her guest, and Adjdaak preferred not to think that she would be so uncultured. He selected some clothes that were not too binding on his human body, improved the comfort level with a few judicious rips and tears, and came outside feeling very pleased with himself.

In the fresh air, even in this inferior, small-nosed human body, he could sniff out locations of the fiery beverage that the Russian Colonel Grisha habitually brought him as tribute. At this very moment there were people pouring out splashes of a similar liquor in a building to the south and east of his current location. Quite likely they were some of his own worshippers, pouring out libations. How pleased and surprised they would be when he appeared amongst them!

There was a real human approaching his spot on the sidewalk now – no, two of them, an adult pushing a small cart that contained a hatchling. The adult one was giving him a very strange look; the little hatchling gazed into his eyes and clapped its hands with evident pleasure.

He had better get out of here before this human also tried to make him responsible for watching its young. "*Arqi djlashdrm!q,*" Adjdaak said hastily.

Rena Sinclair seriously considered fainting when the weirdly costumed guy in front of her disappeared into thin air, but she had Kevin to think of. And Kevin had begun wailing as though somebody had stolen his favorite binky. "There, there," Rena tried to comfort him, kneeling beside the stroller, "see, here's Unicorn Binky." She proffered a rubber pacifier attached to a small stuffed unicorn and Kevin batted it away angrily.

Sadly, by the time that Kevin learned enough human speech to explain that he was crying for the glowing golden jewels in the strange man's face, he would have forgotten all about topaz eyes and disappearing dragon-men.

12. Playing dragon

I'd learned a couple of things by checking out the back yard and the little screened-in back porch that we used as a laundry and cat litter room. When Thalia arrived, complete with a robot-snake mage around her waist and a baby on her hip, I filled her in.

"Either he's been here, or somebody broke into the house before Rukshana and I got home. The objects that used to be my back door locks are now pathetic scraps of metal. I found them lying on the concrete walkway." After a careful, gingerly touch to make sure they weren't hot, I'd scooped up the pitiful remains and put them on the kitchen table. They didn't look like the work of some random burglar with a crowbar. They looked like the trail of destruction that tended to follow casual use of dragon speech.

"And," I said while Mr. M. uncoiled himself and slithered around the scraps, humming and buzzing to himself, "he didn't take his clothes, because I threw them in with a load of laundry last night and forgot about them. I just put the stuff in the dryer when I got home. So presumably he is in dragon form, and I guess we *could* just wait for the hysteria on the evening news to tell us where he's gone." Not that I really wanted to do it that way, but I hadn't come up with anything better.

Aleksi grabbed one of the lock fragments and wailed when Thalia took it out of his chubby little fist before he could stick it into his mouth. "Really," she said crossly to Mr. M., "the least you could do is keep that junk out of his reach."

Rukshana ducked down in her chair, then pretended to leap up over the baby with her hands flapping at the sides of her neck. Aleksi stopped crying to laugh and Rukshana did it again.

"How clever," Thalia said. "Where did you learn how to do that?"

"We call it 'playing dragon,'" Rukshana said between leaping and pouncing. "Careful, baby! Dragon will eat you!"

Aleksi thought this was the funniest thing he'd ever heard.

The dryer buzzed at me through the delighted giggling. For lack of anything more constructive to do, I piled the clean, dry clothes into a basket and carried them through towards my bedroom to put away. Rukshana took Aleksi from Thalia and started another game, a complicated jigging dance on her lap punctuated by periodically opening her knees and pretending to let the baby fall through to the floor. "Well, I never," Thalia said, looking at the two of them with a slightly bemused air. "Talk about cultural universals."

"Huh?" The little Taklan song Rukshana was singing, all about jumping across mountain peaks and sliding down on the ice, didn't sound at all familiar to me.

"Didn't you ever sing that to your cousins?"

"Thalia, I don't *know* any little songs about snow and ice. And if I did, nobody in Beeville would have known what I was singing about!"

"Oh, well. Different words, I guess. But you know my kid brother Andy? He's quite a bit younger than the rest of us. I used to play that with him. 'Trot, trot to Boston,'" she sang quietly, "'Trot, trot to Lynn, you better watch *out* or you might fall *in*!' Only I didn't realize Aleksi was old enough to enjoy it."

I paused at the bedroom door and listened to Rukshana for a moment. Yep. Same tune, different words. And same climax, as she pretended to drop the frantically giggling baby.

Cultural universals? I supposed that if babies loved being dropped so much, it made sense that the same kinds of games would develop everywhere.

Thalia trailed after me into the bedroom and stared around her. I started automatically taking clothes from the basket to fold them.

Cath Palug was on top of the tall bookcase beside my bed. It was one of his favorite perches, a place where he could be quiet and invisible until I made the mistake of lying down where he could leap down onto my vulnerable body with all four feet extended. But he wasn't being quiet and invisible now; he was pacing to and fro and hissing, and his fur stood out all over him like a full-body halo.

Looking at the shambles in the bedroom, I felt like doing some hissing myself. "Looks like somebody broke in after all."

"How can you tell?" Thalia asked.

I waved my hand. "Look at this mess! My lingerie is falling out of its drawers, half my clothes have been tossed onto the bed, and my shoes are scattered all over the floor."

"Oh. That's not, not normal?"

"What, do you think I leave my things in this kind of mess all the time?"

"I do," she confessed.

"Oh. Well… I don't straighten my dresser top every morning or organize my shoes by heel height or anything, you know, *compulsive*. But I like my clothes and I do usually hang them up or fold them into drawers.

"*Somebody* has been in here since I left for work this morning. They've pulled half my clothes off their hangers and rooted through my drawers. Not to mention apparently trying on *one* of every pair of shoes I possess." I rescued my favorite jeans and the skirt to my beige linen suit from the bed and hung them back in the closet. "The only thing is, what could they have been looking for?"

Last fall the answer would have been obvious: that little green notebook full of somebody's field notes on the Language of the Dragon, or as the researcher had called it, Alt-Shaimaki, the old language of Shaimak. Or, as I was beginning to think of it, the dragon language. But that notebook had come to a fiery end, thanks to Adjdaak, and the man who'd been behind all the attempts to steal it had gone mad and walked off an ice cliff in the Pamir Mountains. Nobody, not even Michael, knew that I'd photographed the notebook pages and saved the data on a thumb drive before the original was destroyed. So, logically, nobody should have been breaking into my house to steal the thumb drive.

Besides, whoever had tossed my bedroom had clearly not been looking for anything that small. They hadn't gotten into anything but the clothes closet, the shoe rack, and a couple of drawers of underwear. They hadn't even touched the gun safe.

Reserving the bit about the thumb drive as something she didn't need to know, I went through my analysis of the mess with Thalia. She nodded slowly. "In fact," she said when I'd finished, "you might think they were just looking for something to wear."

"Yes, but nobody who just wanted to steal some clothes would take the time to make this much of a mess."

"Mmm."

"You've had an idea, haven't you? Spill!"

"Well… You did mention that Adjdaak doesn't seem to quite understand all the rules of our culture. Since his jeans and shirt were in the wash, do you suppose he was looking for something else to wear?"

"In my closet?"

Thalia grinned. She seemed to be enjoying this. "I bet you never explained the finer points of men's and women's clothing to him. Why would you? Everybody in Austin except you wears jeans all the time anyway."

I groaned. "I do have some black jeans – no, he's not wearing those, I see them in the corner. Anyway, everything I own would be way too tight on his human form."

"Unless he picked something loose and flowing. You do wear a lot of lacy blouses and full skirts." Thalia was definitely enjoying the situation. "He wouldn't be able to fasten the waistband, but with enough ripping and tearing he would be able to sort of drape one of your outfits over him."

I groaned. "I guess I'll have to put everything away again so I can tell what's missing."

"That'll take *forever*!"

Actually it took less than fifteen minutes. I guess that since Thalia, by her own admission, never hangs anything up, she has no idea how quickly one can restore order to a closet if it's what you're used to having. Before Rukshana had tired of keeping Aleksi amused, Thalia and I had a pretty good idea of what to look for: a six-foot blond male with glowing eyes and very strong fingernails, wearing an off-the-shoulder red lace peasant blouse and a matching lace-trimmed skirt over my navy-blue Reeboks.

"What an awful outfit," Thalia said.

"Hey. It looks pretty good on me... at least I thought it would, when I bought it. Well, anyway, I thought I could get away with *one* red blouse."

"Didn't work?"

"Picked up and amplified the red in my hair, and made me look totally washed-out otherwise. It may work better with Adjdaak's complexion."

"I wasn't thinking about the color. I was picturing him swishing around in all that lace."

"You think people might get the wrong impression?"

Thalia shrugged. "Even if they decide he's a cross-dresser with terrible fashion sense—"

"Hey. I *liked* that outfit!" Even if it didn't work with my coloring.

She gave me an amused look. "Oh, okay. What do I know about fashion, anyway? I stick with jeans and classic rock T-shirts. My point was just that human form, however oddly dressed, is probably better than having him wandering around Austin in dragon form. I just wish I knew where he'd gone."

I sank down on the edge of the bed. "Oh, so do I. He could get himself killed out there, and then..."

Thalia turned white. "Don't even think that! How could we ever explain to his people?"

Selfishly, I had been thinking more about the question of how I would ever get Rukshana back where she belonged without the dragon's help. But Thalia had a point. Of sorts.

"Well, I don't suppose Taklanistan would declare war on us over a missing dragon. It would be too much like *The Mouse that Roared*, don't you think?"

"I *wish* we knew where he'd gone," she said again. She plopped down beside me on the bed, knocking over a neat little stack of underwear that I had rescued from a tangled heap and folded to put away. Mr. M., who'd found himself a cozy nest between the camisoles and the matching panties, fell out of the stack and complained that we were interrupting his nap.

"Why do you not go after Adjdaak, instead of sitting here and complaining about him?"

"We would, if we had any idea where to go."

"Cannot you smell him?"

After a digression about the general inferiority of humans to other intelligent life-forms, and the particular inadequacy of our nasal sensors, Mr. M. volunteered to transport us to Adjdaak's current location.

"How?" Thalia demanded. "We haven't seen it, so I can't use Brouwer teleportation to… I mean…" She tried to catch my eye. I carefully stared out the window. As long as I don't know exactly what Thalia does, I don't have to worry about how she does it. I have enough problems dealing with the magical potential of the dragon's language; I refuse to even consider the possibility that there are other, completely different magical systems out there.

"I can use the same commands that he invoked to transport himself thither," said Mr. M.

"Is that safe? For you?" I had to ask.

He raised his front end up several inches and admired his own reflection in the shining scales of his prosthetic body. "If use of the dragon's speech harms you, it must be that your brains are too weak to accommodate the alternative reality of that language. *My* brain will suffer no injury whatsoever."

"Okay," Thalia said, "take Sienna and do what you can to tamp down whatever disaster Adjdaak is creating. I'll take Aleksi home." She muttered something about never again leaving the baby with a nonhuman Pamiri villager and a paranormal reptile as babysitters.

***

The room where Adjdaak found himself was more like a house in his native village than anywhere else he'd been since escaping that village with Rukshana. This had both good and bad points. On one claw, the atmosphere was comfortingly familiar: dark room, too many humans in the space, a delicious smell like spilled vodka reaching his nostrils. On the other claw, he did not like being inside enclosed spaces that were too small for him to shift back into dragon form.

At least these humans were properly respectful. They didn't stare; their eyes slid over him and down to the floor, and they stood or sat in quiet murmuring groups.

And best of all, the smell of cooked meat blended with that of their local substitute for vodka. Adjdaak even recognized the native viands on the plate nearest him. He picked up the plate and tossed the contents into his mouth – then scrambled to pick up the bits that had missed their target. He had momentarily forgotten how small and unimpressive a human-form mouth was compared to his own magnificent serrated jaws.

Already, then, a disadvantage to being stuck in this small house. He would have to take the mincing little bites allowed by this form, ingesting little more than half a *cheeseburger* at a time.

"This offering is pleasing to me," he told the man whose plate he'd taken, allowing the refulgence of his golden eyes to glow upon the worshipper in sign of approbation. "Your servants may bring me more of the *cheeseburger*."

"You going to let him dis you like that, Gordo?" demanded one of the other peasants, a short man with shoulders almost as broad as Adjdaak's own. He was not nearly as well dressed as Adjdaak, wearing only a thin white sleeveless shirt compared to Adjdaak's impressive red lace frills. But then, was it not a part of human customs that the peasants should not compete with their betters in matters of costume?

Adjdaak remembered Sienna's injunctions about being civil and talking to the peasants as though they were his equals – ridiculous idea, that, but he would follow the custom of the country. "Please, what is to *dis*?" he inquired.

The burly man shouldered his way towards Adjdaak. "You trying to be funny? Because, see, this here is Tank's bar, and Tank –" he tapped his own chest – "don't like your kind in here, even before you got grabby with Gordo's food."

"Ah. You are Tank? My pleasure. You may call me Adjdaak."

"I don't call your kind anything at all," Tank rumbled in a low but pleasing voice. It almost sounded as though he were clashing rocks together in his throat. Adjdaak felt a moment of joy. At last, someone whose voice reminded him of home and his beautiful mate!

"I dunno about the other side of town," Tank went on, "I guess anything goes around that university. But around here, we think a man oughta be a man and a woman oughta be a woman."

Adjdaak frowned. "That would seem to be a self-evident proposition. What alternative could you possibly suggest?"

"You trying to be funny?" Tank growled again, sounding even more like a speaker of Dragon. He flexed his arms and made the tattoos over his biceps ripple up and down.

"No, I am trying to understand what you are saying."

Tank sighed and pointed to a peasant who was half slumped over the bar. "Nobody oughta come in here wearing a dress unless they look like that, see?"

Adjdaak studied the recommended model carefully. He himself did not find the shape either imposing or attractive, but there should be no difficulty in emulating it. Assuming that its grotesque bulges were among the features meeting with Tank's approval, he could even improve upon it. "That is what you wish? I shall do what I can."

The shift from one type of peasant to another was so trivial, he did not even need a worded command to achieve it. He felt a welcome loosening of the skirt where it had constricted his waist, complemented by a new pressure in his chest area where Sienna's red lace blouse was strained to its limits.

Tank's eyes rolled up, showing incongruous crescents of white in his tanned face. He took a step backward, bumped into the bar, and reached out without looking away from Adjdaak's chest. "Shorty! Hit me."

The very tall, thin man who responded to 'Shorty' did not, as Adjdaak was expecting, obey Tank's request to hit him. Instead he splashed something that smelled *delicious* into a small glass and set it in Tank's hand. Tank drained the contents and pushed the glass back over the bar. "Hit me again."

He received a refill, and Adjdaak decided that he had just learned a new and very useful idiom.

"I did not see that," Tank belched on an alcohol-rich exhalation. "I didn't see nothing, I ain't been here, I… I think I'll put some more burgers on the grill."

"Indeed, that would be a most welcome offering," Adjdaak said. The single cheeseburger he'd had so far was more of an appetizer than a meal. To his disappointment, Tank backed through a swinging door at the end of the bar without repeating the promise to grill more cheeseburgers. Gordo followed him.

Adjdaak sighed. "I am beginning to work up an appetite, pandering to the requests of ignorant peasants." He remembered the new idiom. "Shorty, hit me."

"Show me your money first."

Adjdaak frowned, confused. "The other peasant did not have money."

"Tank? He owns the place, man."

"But then..."

A peasant who had, to all appearance, been asleep with his head on the table stirred, saw Adjdaak, and sat up, wide-eyed. "Hey, Shorty, that's no way to treat a lady!" He wove an unsteady path around the obstacles of chairs and tables and fetched up against the bar and nearly against Adjdaak. "*Hel*-lo, gorgeous, can I buy you a *caballito*?"

Adjdaak worked through the language shift and thought that over. "I thank you, but I do not presently desire a small horse, though the offer is generous indeed."

The peasant laughed gustily. His breath had a delectable aroma of garlic. Pre-seasoned human, now, that would be a treat! But as for what the peasant had actually offered... well, horse was edible in an emergency, but he strongly preferred goat or sheep. Or pizza, or cheeseburgers... "This is a wonderful country," Adjdaak sighed, sniffing the tantalizing aromas wafting from the kitchen.

"Damn straight it is!" The peasant slapped him on the shoulder. Before Adjdaak could flambé him for such presumption, the man turned to the bartender and demanded a "shot" for himself and one for his new friend here.

"Try the tequila," he suggested, raising his own glass towards Adjdaak.

Adjdaak downed the clear liquid in one gulp. Ah! It was not exactly vodka, but it had the same latent fire. He exhaled happily, not bothering to control the smoke coming out of his nostrils or the tongues of fire leaping out of his mouth.

"Holy shit," shouted the peasant who'd invited him to drink, "will ya look at that? Real fire water, huh, Shorty?"

The other peasants in the room had been propelled into sudden motion. They seemed to be trying to get behind chairs, tables, and each other, creating a confused, struggling knot.

A thud to his right distracted Adjdaak. He looked over the bar and saw that the man called Shorty had thrown himself to the floor behind the bar. He had not, however, taken the bottle of not-vodka with him. Adjdaak upended the open bottle over his mouth, then, remembering his manners, offered it to the peasant who'd first given him a drink.

That was *excellent* fuel; he hadn't felt this warmth in his belly since he and Rukshana left Shaimak. Adjdaak relieved the growing heat with a long, happy sigh of golden and blue flame that was mirrored across the bar. Oh – of course. Wood burned so easily; he'd seldom had to worry about that during his century of living in a treeless mountain landscape where humans had few objects made of wood. Here, by contrast, they seemed to use wood as though it were as common as stone or snow. A little more fire trickled out of Adjdaak's nostrils and set a chair alight.

"*Adjdaak!* What do you think you're doing now?"

It was Sienna, looking pale and flustered, with the turtle-snake mage draped over her shoulders. The mirror behind the bar showed her looking positively fragile next to Adjdaak's current exuberant form. She grabbed his arm and he winced; his dragon forelegs were the most fragile part of his body, probably the only part that could feel pain from something as trivial as a girl's grip. "Never mind, come on!"

"Why?"

"Don't be stupid." She looked back at the people tumbling into the bar. There were shouts, and lights flashing, and even as he watched Tank came storming out of the back room and threw a punch at one of the newcomers. Adjdaak was in no hurry to abandon such an entertaining scene.

"I am not stupid," he said stiffly.

"Okay. You're brilliant. At least, you're sharp enough to understand that you don't want to go to jail. Right?"

"Where is *jale*?"

"It's a place way too cramped to let you change back into dragon form. We have to get out of here!"

"Oh well, in that case," he conceded, "*B#z vlaad udjy.*"

13. Off with their heads

Because it was Adjdaak who'd spoken, I was spared the blinding headache that usually accompanied my own attempts to use his language. What I experienced instead was scarcely less disorienting. Color and form drained out of the world like liquids out of a tilting vessel; only Adjdaak, beside me, kept his outlines and color. That red lace blouse was even more blinding in this swirling chaos of nothingness. I had time to think that it had been a really poor fashion choice on my part; then, that it didn't matter because Adjdaak had destroyed most of the seams; and then it occurred to my befuddled brain that this was probably not the best time for a lengthy meditation on my color and fashion sense.

The cold focused my attention on more important matters. What had been a warm early spring evening in Austin was turning into a breath of Arctic air. First I was all over goosebumps, then my toes and fingers started to ache with the cold, and then Adjdaak made an impatient noise that sounded like, "Huh!"

He followed that up with, "*Y#q Shaimak'd,*" and then, as the cold dissipated, "*B#z vlaad udjy Taksus'd.*"

My fingers and toes defrosted all in a breathtaking swoop, and I fell onto the stacks of folded clothes on the bed in my own bedroom. Beside me, Adjdaak sat down hard on the mattress.

"So, *'d* is a particle of location in your language, is it?"

"For a human, you have a very strange reaction to being magically rescued," Adjdaak said, sounding distinctly grumpy. He pried my fingers loose from his forearm.

"You'd rather I screamed and fainted? Anyway, it was more me rescuing you, don't you think?"

"You are a very *argumentative* human, are you not?"

"I'm not nearly as bad that way as Michael is. You don't know how lucky you are." And I just might scream and faint if I thought over what had happened. So I thought about what I'd just learned about dragon speech instead. I *understood* language structure. It was comfortingly familiar.

"It got really cold there for a minute. We were headed to the wrong version of 'home,' weren't we? All the way back to the mountains of Taklanistan? So you said *Y#q*, which is a general-purpose negative, right? And then *Shaimak*, your home, only with a new ending: *Shaimak'd*. And then you said again that we are becoming at home." A belated sense of caution prevented me from repeating the words, because they were a complete sentence. Sentences in Adjdaak's language had consequences, and the last thing I wanted was to invoke the power of the language. "And," I finished triumphantly, "you followed that with *Taksus'd*. Clearly you were saying that we were not home in Shaimak, we were home in Texas – it's TEK-sas, not TAK-sus, by the way – and that *'d* is a suffix meaning something like 'in'. Or 'at'. Or 'near'. Can you use it with anything besides place names? Would you say *udjy'd* for 'at home'?"

Working out language details always makes me feel calmer, like at least I'm in control of some part of my environment. But Adjdaak didn't want to play. He growled that nobody would say *udjy'd* because it was redundant, and lucky for me that it wasn't a real construction. Didn't I remember what speaking his language could do to weak human brains? Where did I get this compulsion to play with fire, anyway?

"Gee, I don't know," I said. "Perhaps because having you around means constantly playing with fire? Literally?"

Adjdaak announced that he was going to rest in the back yard and I could bring him some food and some of that not-vodka liquid later.

"Maybe," I hedged. I felt that Adjdaak had soaked up enough of my time and energy for a while. Then again, I didn't want to turn him loose on Austin to get his own supplies, so a food run was probably in order – later.

Adjdaak shed the clothes he'd reduced to rags, went out to the back yard and began grooming his dragon form. I automatically picked up the remnants of the red lace blouse and coordinating skirt, started to drop them in the laundry hamper, changed course and stuffed them into the trash. So much for that particular fashion disaster. Adjdaak and I needed to have a serious talk about clothing before he helped himself to an outfit I actually liked.

That could wait, though. Right now I needed to prep; I was scheduled for a full day of one-on-one tutoring sessions tomorrow. I had one math graduate student wanting to use French for his proficiency requirement, another who wanted Russian, a couple of history students who were studying German, and a sociologist and a political scientist who were optimistically trying to get their departments to accept Spanish for one of their proficiency requirements.

Before meeting with all those clients, I needed to think about how I was going to tackle the challenges involved. I felt pretty sure I could tell whether the history students were translating papers from *Historische Zeitschrift* accurately, but the other subjects had their own pitfalls. Mr. M. had zipped off home as soon as we were safely back here, before I could send a message: I had forgotten to talk to Thalia about getting some technical support for the math students, and I direly needed that. It would be hard for me to evaluate how well a student translated something out of a French or Russian math book, given that the subject matter was Greek to me. (Except, of course, that I can read Greek reasonably well. I'll take Greek over calculus any day.) As for the soft "sciences," I suspected that none of the papers in journals like *Estudios Sociologicos* actually said anything at all, so how would I know if my clients grasped the intended meaning? The only sociology textbooks I'd encountered in college had the intellectual consistency of library paste.

There was a lot to think through before I even made introductory lesson plans for tomorrow. So, naturally, I wandered out to the living room to watch the evening news. It would be interesting to see if there was anything about a mysterious fire in a sleazy bar south of the river. At least I'd gotten Adjdaak out of there before any journalists with cameras arrived…I hoped. Some new people *had* been coming in as we left, but surely it would be too much of a coincidence if they were journalists slumming in Shorty's? I made a mental note of one more thing to ask Adjdaak: just how much control did he have over his human form? I'd now seen him as a ripped six-foot male and as an exuberantly busty six-foot female, both versions with blond hair and topaz eyes. Could he alter his form to that of, say, a short guy with dark hair and eyes? And would he consider doing that for the next few days, just until I was sure nobody would recognize either of his previous human shapes from the bar?

The fire didn't make the early evening news; I didn't know about the associated problems it had created until later, when the ten o'clock news came on. And not being distracted by that foreknowledge, I actually did manage to make a few notes about tomorrow's tutoring sessions after I turned off the TV.

Once I tamped down the panicked voice screaming *I don't know what I'm doing!* it got easier. I just had to remember that the clients were probably even worse off. At least I was comfortable in French, German, Russian and Spanish; that put me well ahead of them, didn't it? Also, all of these would be introductory sessions. I didn't have to start them reading randomly chosen pages from foreign journals in their field just yet, in fact they'd almost certainly be overwhelmed if I did so. Tomorrow's focus would be on evaluating each student's capacity and needs.

From my years of casually tutoring languages to pick up a little extra cash, I could already guess that a couple of my new clients would need nothing more than hand-holding and plenty of practice to build up their confidence that they wouldn't actually expire on the spot when handed an unfamiliar journal article to translate and explain. A couple of the others would show up with a death-grip on transcripts showing that they had actually passed a French or Russian or Spanish class as undergraduates, and hoping that I could sprinkle some magic dust on the transcripts turning them into the required proof of language proficiency. And the rest... The rest would be where I earned my money. The Americans who just *knew* they could never learn a foreign language, no how, no way, and were coming to me to have that belief verified so they could give up on the careers they'd worked so hard at and go home without facing the dragon of Language.

Those were, actually, my most rewarding clients. I really loved the process of dismantling their old fears and seeing my students blossom as they grasped that French, for instance, was not a medieval torture system designed by the Inquisition but a language so easy to use that hundreds of thousands of little French pre-schoolers jabbered away in it without ever getting stuck.

But that was often a long, slow process, and proficiency exams would be happening in ten weeks. I should have started the business earlier in the semester. Or later. Or – well, any time, actually, except *right now*!

"Jam tomorrow, or jam yesterday, but never jam today?" Michael suggested when, on his arrival, I practically threw myself at him, a gibbering mass of insecurities.

"*Huh?*"

"Didn't you ever read *Alice in Wonderland*? Or maybe that bit is in *Through the Looking Glass*."

"Mom read them to me, but I was six years old. I don't remember that much."

"You really should read them again," he said while unpacking the plastic bags he'd brought over onto the kitchen table. "Especially now, because you remind me of the Red Queen."

"Off with their heads?"

"Running twice as fast to stay in the same place."

"Oh." I sat and watched him unpack. There seemed to be an awful lot of Styrofoam containers.

"Barbecue," he said, nodding at the biggest box. "Adjdaak likes a lot of meat, doesn't he?"

"Adjdaak," I said darkly, "can damned well go out and barbecue his own meat for all I care. Do you know what he did today while he was supposed to be watching Thalia's baby?"

I wasn't nearly through complaining when my phone played a merry little tune meant to remind me that it was time for the late news. While Adjdaak enjoyed a small mountain of barbecue, I settled down in the living room again hoping for a very, very dull local news hour. Michael brought bowls, spoons and ice cream. "I know you like crazy flavors," he announced, looking proud of himself. I had a brief moment's giddy expectation of the new mix from

Amy's Ice Cream – Cointreau chocolate mint swirl – before he dashed my hopes by continuing, "So I got vanilla *and* strawberry. Which do you want?"

"I think I'll go wild and mix them," I said, swallowing my slight disappointment. I *had* already learned that Michael doesn't understand ice cream.

After which, battered by the lead story on the local news station, I ate way too much strawberry and vanilla ice cream. Oh, yes, the fire and fight at Shorty's had made the news. The station's talking heads made a big deal of the mysterious Lady in Red but I noticed that they didn't actually show any pictures of her breathing fire. *Thank you, God.* They did, however, have an interview with Tank.

And Tank… had pictures. And quite a story.

He'd looked out back just as Adjdaak and I made our getaway, and he claimed to have seen Adjdaak changing to dragon form. He did not, thank God, have pictures of that. But he'd taken a snapshot of Adjdaak inside the bar, as the (not exactly a) Lady in Red, and he claimed to have seen him – her? –it? breathing fire.

"I don't suppose you have a picture of *that*," the interviewer said sadly.

Tank shook his head and I breathed more easily.

But he did, he announced, have a picture of the Lady in Red's confederate. The image that flashed upon the screen was so wild-eyed and disheveled that for a moment I didn't recognize it; could have been any crazy woman with no fashion sense.

Then I groaned and reached for Michael's bowl, which still held a lump of gently melting vanilla ice cream. *Softening me up with the small mercies, were you, Lord?*

"Why don't I ever comb my hair before going out to rescue people?" I bitterly enquired of the ceiling.

"Could be worse," Michael said, wrapping a comforting arm around my shoulders. "If you recall, you spent half an hour with combs and various products to tame your hair before we took the picture we're using on the website. Nobody could possibly associate *that* impeccably dressed and made-up lady with *this* picture."

That would have been more comforting if I hadn't felt that the no-makeup, hair-bursting-free version was a lot closer to my everyday self.

14. Something to believe in

All that sugar should have stimulated my brain, but it was Michael who came up with the next obvious step: more meat, he said. If the Russians were looking for Adjdaak while waving a picture of me, then the last place Adjdaak should be tomorrow was my office. Rukshana should probably go in with us – the Russians didn't know about her – but Adjdaak should lie low.

When I pointed out that being inconspicuous was not exactly Adjdaak's forte, Michael said, "Wait here," and disappeared into the night. I spent forty minutes nibbling on my fingernails before I heard his car pull up outside again, and he never did tell me how he persuaded a butcher to open up his market at eleven p.m.

"A lot of stuff passes through Joe's that isn't exactly approved," was all he would say.

"Ick. Do you mean I've been eating horse meat?"

"No no no, nothing like that. If he *does* sell horse meat, it's to the pet food trade. Pet food manufacturers buy a lot of animal protein that would make you say, 'ick,' and they aren't that particular about where they get it. Do you think Adjdaak would be willing to eat this stuff raw?"

He wasn't, but he did consent to limit the preparation to searing the ragged cuts of meat lightly all over. That got me a call from Jenn, my next-door nosy neighbor, asking whether I knew that there were children playing with fireworks in my back yard. I told her not to worry, my boyfriend was setting up a propane grill.

"Well, can't he wait until morning?"

"He's almost done," I said, and didn't quite hang up on her when she went off on a tangent about how outdoor grilling was bad for the environment. I extricated myself tactfully and joined Michael in chatting with Adjdaak to distract him from the fact that some mere human who hadn't even been introduced to him dared to critique his cooking style.

Adjdaak would probably have pigged out on all that meat anyway, but Michael made it a sure thing by spinning a story about its being donations from worshippers to express their delight in the honor of a dragon visiting Austin. It was one in the morning before he crunched up the last messy mouthful of bloodied and singed bones and announced his intention of taking a short nap to digest the offerings. After which, he said, he would… probably… reward his worshippers… with…

The snoring of an extremely well-fed dragon, in case you were wondering, sounds an awful lot like a dragon's conversation in his native language: noises like somebody breaking up a large rock pile, interspersed with disgusting belches. "What do you suppose he plans to do for his worshippers?" I whispered to Michael when we were sure Adjdaak was truly asleep. "And how can we stop him?"

Michael shook his head and drew me back into the house. "We'll cross that bridge when we come to it. This just bought us a little time. Rukshana says this was about three times as much meat as he ever got at one time in Shaimak, so digesting it ought to keep him quiescent for at least a day. I'll spend tomorrow figuring out how to persuade him to go home."

"Good luck with that!"

Michael's face looked almost as rock-like as Adjdaak in disguise. "There's no decent alternative. He can hardly stay at this house, now that the Russians know he's associated with you. In fact, he should leave Austin altogether."

"I'm not totally sure I want to stay at this house either!"

"I'll be with you tonight."

"You and what army?"

"Oh, relax. Don't you have lesson plans to write?"

"Did that before the late news."

"Oh, well, maybe I can think of some other way to distract you. Is

Rukshana still sleeping on your bedroom floor?"

It turned out that she had moved into the front room where I'd thought Adjdaak would be staying. She was fast asleep on the floor of that room, looking a bit like a recumbent sunflower with her bright hair spilling out of the cocoon she'd made from Aunt Milly's green and gold Jacob's Ladder quilt, and I didn't wake her up to ask what had prompted this move.

I was afraid she'd giggle.

It was very late, and I should have been thinking only of getting a decent night's sleep before tomorrow's tutoring marathon, but Michael distracted me from that as well as from worries about the dragon. When I did fall asleep, I slept extremely well; his techniques of distraction were good for that.

I'm told that after thirty, five hours of deep sleep is no longer an adequate substitute for eight hours of normal sleep. Fortunately, I'm still three years away from that deadline. I woke feeling brisk, confident and cheerful about the oncoming day.

Granted, the fact that Adjdaak's snores were still rumbling through the yard helped. So did the large cup of black coffee Michael offered me as a bribe to get up. I even made it to the kitchen and put some bread in the toaster.

"You need a real breakfast before a day as long as this one promises to be," he said, pulling a carton of eggs out of the fridge.

"No time."

"Sit. This won't take long."

"Gotta get to the office."

"You can't leave without Rukshana, and she's not dressed yet. *Sit*! Eat!"

I sat and ate.

Today, I was glad of my snap decision to use Rukshana in the front office. I had essentially zero time between tutoring sessions to manage the ongoing business of signing up and scheduling the new clients who kept showing up. And she had applied herself to the magic of modern technology with impressive results; she might not have quite realized her promise to know "everything," but she was certainly competent to enter data into the computer system Michael had devised, as long as she had time to type with two fingers and search for the right keys. She was also able to print out the resulting schedules, and to send automated notices to tutors for the new languages that today's clients were requesting help with.

My first meeting, with the math graduate student who had come for help with French reading proficiency, ran ten minutes overtime and used up my chance for a coffee break. Good thing Michael had fueled me with scrambled eggs and extra-dark roast. Rukshana was on the phone when I finished this, but she waved at me and used hand signals to send the next client back.

Two Russian journals and one French textbook later, I had half a legal pad's worth of scrawled notes on how to proceed with my first four reading proficiency students, an empty stomach, and a reporter in the front room.

"Sienna Brown!" Fern Monteith cocked her head at me and shot an inquiring glance my way when I surfaced to get coffee and crackers. "I just stopped by to find out if you had any comment on the picture."

"Huh?" My head was buzzing with Russian palatalized consonants and French nasalized syllables. My clients seemed to feel it was cruel and unusual to expect them to actually *pronounce* the strange foreign sentences they were mangling in translation. I saw the matter differently. If they couldn't *say* the sentences, how could they get past word-by-word translations to *feel* the meaning?

"The picture of you," Monteith clarified, "from that bar fight last night."

I shook my head. "Not me. Coincidence."

"And what about your fire-breathing friend?"

I shook my head again. "No comment, sorry, busy day." Whew! Here came Rukshana. I gave her a meaningful look, jerked my chin Taklan-style to indicate the *Grackle* woman, and withdrew to let Rukshana get rid of the pestiferous reporter.

Once safely back in one of the little tutoring cubicles, I experimented with the office phone system. Not only did it work, Rukshana answered and promised to send back a sandwich and a fruit bowl as soon as she was free. She must be having a little trouble getting rid of Monteith.

The sociologist and the political scientist were only trying to pass Spanish proficiency exams, which for anybody who grew up in Texas really shouldn't have been an insurmountable challenge. Sadly, they combined a high degree of respect for their own intellectual prowess with a degree of language insensitivity that I hadn't encountered since dragging Thalia through French irregular verbs. Some people's brains seemed to be actively resistant to language forms. Even Floss and Blossom were able to acquire a couple of new vocabulary words in an hour and a half tutoring session. These two grad students were apparently too smart for that.

After three exhausting hours of working with first the sociologist and then the political scientist, a couple of practical problems with the organization of my fledgling business became clear to me.

First, I was going to have to hire supplemental tutors even for the languages that I myself was competent to teach, because I didn't have time to personally drill every student who needed help in these highly popular European languages.

Second, the scheduling program needed to be set up so that I couldn't casually give up my lunch hour no matter how dire the need, because Rukshana never had brought me any food and now I had a hunger headache as well as a pile of new registrations to look over.

I sat at the double desk in the tutoring cubicle, dithering about what to do next. Advertise for more tutors? Cancel somebody's scheduled session for tomorrow so I'd have time to grab a bite in the middle of the day? Enter my notes from today's sessions into the computer?

The sound of laughter from the front room filtered through to me. Good, Rukshana was still here, hence not out somewhere getting into trouble. Bad, she had apparently forgotten all about getting food for her starving boss.

The thought of food concentrated my mind wonderfully. I needed to do something about my low blood sugar immediately. Then maybe I'd be intelligent enough to tackle all the other tasks awaiting my attention. The only thing I needed to decide right now was, did I want to smile at Rukshana and build up her self-confidence, or snarl at her for abandoning me to starve? She got upset awfully easily, and a weeping or pouting receptionist wouldn't get me the sandwich I desperately needed.

The smile I had pasted on my face couldn't survive what I saw when I staggered into the front room, though.

Fern Monteith.

Still here after all this time, laughing and chatting freely with Rukshana. Didn't the woman have any real reporting to do?

I let one hand fall on Rukshana's shoulder. She jumped and squealed and then she and Monteith both giggled.

"What part of *no comment* didn't you understand, Ms. Monteith?"

"Oh, that was your statement, Sienna. Miss Rukshana has given me a most interesting interview. I think my editor would like to see an in-depth feature exploring how a young woman from such a different culture has adapted to life in America."

"She's just visiting," I said. "And the culture isn't all that different." Well, not in some respects anyway. "Her people speak a Farsi dialect called Taklan. That's an Indo-European language." Actually these days we'd classify it as Indo-Iranian, but that wouldn't mean much to Fern.

Sadly, 'Indo-European' didn't mean anything to her either. "A very interesting language, too. She was just telling me how to talk to dragons."

Üks, kaks, kolm. Finally, three of the five Estonian words I know came in handy. "Folklore," I said between my teeth.

"Very *detailed* folklore. The part about how a dragon brought her here, and they're both staying with you, was particularly interesting. It explains your poetic description of dragons' eyes as glowing topazes, which I had been wondering about. You didn't get that from the pictures I shared with you, did you?"

No, and I hadn't gotten much good out of acting like a lady with this pushy reporter. I mentally cast off my social conditioning and set out to get rid of her. "You're going to look like an idiot," I said, "if you insist on reporting the folklore of the High Pamirs as fact. Have you ever seen a dragon?"

"Well, no, but—"

"Haven't you ever heard of double-checking your sources? Go find somebody else from Taklanistan and ask them about dragons! Oh, but you wouldn't want to do that, would you? They'd laugh at you, and there goes your fantastical story."

Fern Monteith's chin somehow got more prominent, and her eyes flashed. "People need something to believe in. If there *were* dragons, why wouldn't they come to Austin?"

"Why would they? This may be hard for somebody who writes for the *Grackle* to grok, but Austin's live music scene is not actually one of the major interspecies attractions of this planet."

"And you know this how?"

I threw up my hands and perched on the corner of Rukshana's desk. I was actually feeling a little too dizzy to keep standing. "Okay. You got me there. Maybe Austin is where Area 51 meets Middle Earth. I'll believe it when you show me the evidence. Forgive me for trying to save you from making an idiot of yourself in the local paper."

"You know the single thing that most convinces me there's something in this dragon story?"

"The desire to believe in something crazy?"

"Your desire to make me stop asking questions about it."

"Oh, ask all the questions you want, lady, but leave me and my staff out of it. We've got a business to run!"

I'd completely dropped counting to three as a way to give me time to think of a polite way to say things, and I had a feeling there wasn't going to be any free publicity for Sienna Language Services in forthcoming issues of the *Grackle*. Michael would be unhappy with me. Well, tough. He could yell at me all he liked, just as long as I got something to eat first.

15. Dragon bait

Sometimes Bogdan wondered why every move he and his confederates made had to be preceded by hours of bickering in whatever squalid room they had found for shelter. More often he wondered why, if their mission was so important to Mother Russia, their budget didn't cover more than a couple of scoped rifles and the cheapest no-tell motel in town. Okay, staying under the Americans' radar meant finding places that took cash and didn't keep records, but did Zhenya *have* to keep putting them in rooms with suspicious stains on the carpet? He was willing to bet that when people like his boss, members of the *nomenklatura*, visited the degenerate capitalist countries, they didn't stay in dingy rooms that smelled of sweet air freshener overlaying much worse things.

Tonight's bickering had begun with all three of them blaming each other for missing this chance to catch up with the dragon. After a bit of whining, the positions became clear.

Kostya felt sure that the busty tramp in the torn red lace outfit had actually been the dragon they were looking for, because of the bar owner's claim to have seen her breathe fire. The pictures of her and her accomplice were up on the TV station's website now, and Kostya had downloaded them.

Zhenya wanted to know why a male dragon would change into the shape of a female human.

Bogdan himself thought the dragon might be female, which made more sense of the shape-shifting. But he also thought that a blurred photo of a disheveled female who *might* have been accompanying the (Not a) Lady in

Red was not a clue that they had any chance of following up.

"Facial recognition algorithms?" Kostya suggested.

"Applied to what data base?"

"Easy." He smirked. "I send the picture to the boss in Nizhny. The boss gets somebody to hack the Austin Police Department's data base. That ditzy looking redhead is bound to have a record. All we need is a name and address to go with the face."

"Fine," Bogdan sighed, "but while we're waiting for the hacker to get back to us, I plan to do something a little more proactive."

"Like what?" Zhenya whined. "You determined to get us arrested?"

"Not planning anything risky," Bogdan said.

"I don't think you've *got* a plan."

"Sure I do. Two words: Dragon. Bait."

It took a few more words than that to convey his plan to the two idiots he'd been lumbered with, but once they got the idea they were all for it. Of course, that didn't mean they quit bickering and whining. It just meant that the bickering shifted from "We can't do anything," to, "Why didn't you do that this morning?"

Actually, it wasn't all that easy to organize the bait for the next morning. Vodka was easy enough to come by, but the other item required them to do some shopping around in East Austin before they located a seller who could get them both the bait and a pickup truck to transport it.

They were in place before dawn, crouched behind the stone tables and benches behind the clearing on the top of the hill. Bogdan personally tethered the goat to a twisted little tree at one side of the clearing. Then he upended the vodka bottle over a large rock with a concave top.

"You didn't have to pour it *all* out," Zhenya whined.

"Shut up. After this works, a grateful nation will give you all the vodka you can drink."

Zhenya thought this over. "I am not sure that our nation has that much vodka. In any case, a bottle in the hand is worth more than…"

"That," said Bogdan coldly, "is why you did not get your hands on this bottle. First things first! Kostya, you *did* find a range and sight in the rifles while Zhenya and I were goat shopping yesterday, yes?"

"Uh, yes?"

Kostya didn't sound that sure. Oh well. When the dragon swooped down to take the goat, it would be so close that even a half-blind moron with shaky hands should be able to hit it. Once it was dead, they would photograph the corpse before taking some small body parts as proof of the kill. Then Bogdan would pour the can of gasoline over the body and burn it, so that the Americans would not even have a corpse to study. That was why he was in charge, he thought ahead. Zhenya and Kostya hadn't understood why he wanted to lug the gas up the hill with them. Idiots.

Bogdan had placed Kostya and Zhenya, with the rifles, behind a massive rectangle of stone that had probably been dragged up to its position to serve as a bench. Since the stone table behind it had an unacceptably narrow base, he himself went behind the corresponding bench on the far side. It wasn't far enough away; he could still hear both the bleating of the tethered goat and the grousing of his nitwit colleagues. Why, they wanted to know, did they always have to be the ones out front with the rifles?

They knew perfectly well why, but Bogdan wasn't going to gratify them by admitting that ever since losing the sight of one eye in a border skirmish his depth perception had been unreliable. On the whole he felt the loss was worth it; that, or else the savagery with which he exacted vengeance on the rebels who'd been foolish enough to shoot at him, had brought him to the attention of his captain. And that in turn had got him detached from the army by a man far senior to Captain Gruzdev, a man who wanted someone to lead what he deemed "sensitive" missions.

The sensitivity involved not being to anybody's feelings, but to his sponsor's need for discretion.

Now Bogdan didn't bother asking Kostya and Zhenya whether they really wanted a man with no depth perception trying to aim one of the rifles. They would probably say, "Yes." And worse – *much* worse – they might think he wanted their pity. So he merely growled, "Army training. Cannon fodder in front, brains to the rear. Or in your case, *dragon* fodder if you don't shoot straight. The monster will probably think that miserable little goat is just an appetizer."

Having thus inculcated a proper state of terrified brutality in the idiots, Bogdan relaxed minutely; just enough to begin worrying about what he'd do if the dragon failed to take the bait. This wasn't like hunting the beasts in the snow-covered wastes of the mountains, where any little change in the landscape attracted their attention; here they were in the middle of a city where people drove monster-sized vehicles at terrifying speeds and casually threw away perfectly good food that would never be allowed to go to waste back home in Nizhny.

A city where even the proletariat carried cell phones that only a man like Bogdan's exalted boss could purchase at home, and where low dive bars sported monstrous flat-screen televisions with no purpose except to replay the Americans' beloved sports matches.

A city where dragons passed for humans until the flames flickered out from the smiling mouth above the red dress.

A city where a cloud scudding across the windy sky could darken the sunshine... *No.* Bogdan thought his heart stopped for a moment. That was no random cloud; it was a shape with outspread, angular wings and a wedge-shaped head on a snaky neck.

A dragon.

His salvation, if only Kostya and Zhenya did not miss.

They *could not* miss at this range. There'd been no need for the scopes, no need to sight in the rifles. The beast that alighted almost on top of the squealing goat was the size of a house. If that moron Kostya could hit the side of a barn with his rifle, he could –

The double *thump* of two suppressor-fitted rifles firing almost simultaneously reverberated within Bogdan's chest as if his heart had given two extra beats to make up for skipping one a moment earlier. A moment later there was a furious roar; a gust of flame washed over the stone benches and Bogdan tried to flatten himself on the rocky ground, flat as a piece of paper, a *wet* piece of paper, sinking into the stones and away from the pain that seared his back. There was an explosion and he discovered that he could, after all, get closer to the ground than he was already.

Then the goat – no. Those screams were much closer to him than the goat had been. They must be coming from Kostya and Zhenya. Bogdan gingerly lifted himself until one eye could just see across the bench that had sheltered him.

By then, Kostya had stopped screaming. He was sitting up on the ground, rocking back and forth, cradling one hand as if something terrible had happened to it. Beside him, Zhenya appeared to be unharmed. He saw Bogdan's movement and scrambled towards him.

"Kostya's hand shattered when his rifle exploded," he told Bogdan. "We have to get him to a doctor."

Bogdan thought briefly about the questions an American hospital would ask and nodded to Zhenya. "You, take your rifle and get back to the car. I'll see to Kostya."

Beyond the bench where Kostya and Zhenya had been hiding, the ground was bare and the small weeds growing on the stony clearing were reduced to blackened shreds. The dragon was gone; so was the goat. Apart from Kostya, now whimpering in a disgusting show of weakness, only the burnt weeds and a scatter of fan-shaped scales, flickering with blue light around their edges, showed that anything out of the ordinary had taken place on that bright, clear morning.

Bogdan dealt with Kostya and began picking his way down the hillside, putting the Tokarev back into his pocket as he went. A pity the pistol hadn't been fitted with a suppressor, but that would have made it too bulky to carry comfortably. If anybody was in earshot, the explosion and the screaming of goats and men would have attracted attention anyway; a single pistol shot hardly added to his vulnerability. Destroying the body with his supply of gas, on the other hand, would have drawn altogether too much attention. And it shouldn't be necessary anyway; a dead man was much less interesting than a dead dragon.

Halfway down the hill, a scantily clad man – doubtless a common laborer — with hairy bare legs poking out of torn shorts accosted him. "Hey, man, you see that?" The man waved a tiny cell phone at him. "I got *pictures*. You get any?"

Bogdan would never understand America. He knew that capitalist oppression had ground down the commoners… but why did the capitalists allow their laborers such expensive toys?

"Nothink to zee up zere," he grunted, but that was inadequate to deter the young man.

"I think I'll take a look anyway." The laborer sniffed. "Smells like you were having a hell of a barbecue up there. Aren't we under fire restrictions until it rains again?"

"Not me." It was roast goat the man was smelling, Bogdan told himself; not roast Russian. Zhenya hadn't been burned that badly.

But the indefatigable commoner posed a dilemma. Bogdan was almost sure he had collected all the dragon's fallen scales, but he might have missed one; he'd had other things to think about. Too, he hadn't taken time to conceal Kostya's body thoroughly, having counted on being well away from this hill before it was discovered. If he let this fool pass, he might find the body. But if he killed him… The Americans could not know who Kostya was; they would think he was one of their lowest class, the homeless men who camped in parks and under bridges. Bogdan felt sure they would expend no more energy than Russian authorities on investigating the death of such a nobody.

The body of an American, though, might not pass unnoticed. Bogdan grunted something unintelligible and hurried on down the hill. If Zhenya was waiting in the car as ordered, they could still be gone before Kostya's body was found. He needed to get back to their room and contact his boss. He had proof now that they would require additional support to complete their mission.

16. Now you see it, now you don't

After the tutoring marathon, I had barely enough energy to shower, grab something to eat and fall into bed. However, I also had to explain to Rukshana why she shouldn't have talked to Fern Monteith about dragons. That did not actually go terribly well. She exclaimed that she'd been trying to help me by keeping the talkative lady out of my way, and then that nobody appreciated her efforts, and nobody understood her, and she wished she was dead. If I hadn't been exhausted I would have felt guiltier about my failure to communicate with her. As it was, I went off to bed muttering testily to myself that I hadn't signed on for parenting a sulky teenager and the sooner Adjdaak took Rukshana back where she belonged the better off we'd all be. It was just as well, really, that Michael hadn't invited himself over tonight; I had no energy left for anybody else, even him. Although I *was* grateful to him for having stuffed Adjdaak until he spent the whole day sleeping and digesting.

A last peek out the back window in the bedroom reassured me. Adjdaak's faintly glowing scales moved up and down in a long, lazy, undulating pattern that I had learned to recognize as "dragon at rest," and his brilliant eyes were closed. I could, I thought, learn to sleep with the background of a dragon's snores; they were actually a reassuring noise. They reassured me that he wasn't off getting into trouble somewhere else.

The alarm tugged me out of bed the next morning at an hour that felt just barely civilized. I scrubbed the sleep out of my eyes and stumbled into the kitchen to pour coffee down my throat so that I'd be awake enough to deal with a second day-long tutoring marathon. This working lifestyle, like taking care of Rukshana, was something else I hadn't consciously signed on for. What ever happened to slow and easy mornings, breakfast at eleven so I didn't have to bother with lunch, quiet afternoons with just enough tutoring appointments or real estate showings to break up the long pleasant silences?

"Deciding to start your own business is what happened," Laura said when I whined to her. She was more awake than I was and had volunteered to cook breakfast for both of us, saying that I'd need fuel for the day ahead and she needed comfort food for her breakup with Duke. Sweets for comfort, protein for fuel: the obvious solution was French toast. And there was even a little of her genuine maple syrup to pour over it.

"That was Michael's idea," I groused, tilting the maple syrup bottle to get a last drop of sweetness on my breakfast. "I just, it was too much trouble to argue with him about it."

"Sienna, doing nothing is also a decision," Laura admonished me. "If you didn't want the hassles of running your own business, you should have stood up to Michael when he first thought of this plan. Now shut up and read the paper until you've had enough coffee to be human."

"We don't take a paper." I reached for my iPad, which is what I actually read when I want to torture myself by checking the news. Actual *news* news, as in the *Austin American-Statesman*, sounded much too grim and dull. I opened up the *Grackle* app instead, tilting the screen slightly away from Laura. She probably was not up for gossip about the bars-and-bands scene right now, and you couldn't really count on the *Grackle* for much else. Maybe there was a nice, feel-good article in the Lifestyle section about relieving stress. Hemp extract? Acupuncture? I was in the mood to buy into the fad of the week, whatever it might be.

I was not in the mood to enjoy the cover story, illustrated as it was by artists' conceptions of their subject. The one saving grace was that, as far as I could tell, none of the artists had actually seen a dragon in the flesh.

"Dragons of the High Lonely Places," Laura read over my shoulder, and I jumped. I'd been so horrified and absorbed in what I was reading that I hadn't noticed her moving around the kitchen to start a new batch of French toast.

"That witch Monteith," I said, only 'witch' wasn't the word I actually used. "She pumped Rukshana for dragon stories while I was busy yesterday, and this is the result."

"The *Grackle* must have thought the story was pretty hot stuff," Laura commented, still reading over my shoulder. "They're usually not in such a rush to get their stuff into print. Given that the only thing that really has to be timely is the club listings. It's not like anybody reads them for news."

"They certainly won't get much of a hard-news following in the future," I said, "not after publishing this nonsense."

"*Is* it nonsense?"

I skimmed the columns of print, missed a few words, bumped up the font size and tried again. "No, as far as I can tell it's a pretty straightforward account of the dragons of the High Pamirs. Solitary lifestyle, very occasional matings, symbiotic relations with nearby villages—"

"Don't tell me Rukshana used the word 'symbiotic'!"

"No, I suspect that was Monteith's contribution. But it's all true. The dragons nest near remote villages and offer their special services in return for an occasional goat, and adolescents like Rukshana put in some time as servant-apprentices to a dragon as part of their education. At least Monteith didn't mention that the 'special services' usually involve warping reality by the use of a magically powerful language. Either Rukshana failed to spill everything, or Monteith has a little common sense." I couldn't decide which was less likely.

Laura bent closer over my shoulder. I could practically hear her squinting to read the fine print under a picture of a medieval stone carving of a dragon. "Put your glasses on, Laura!"

"In a minute… Why did the *Grackle* give so much space to this story? It's not exactly local news."

"Not until you get to the end." For reasons unknown to me, the editor of the *Grackle* had buried at the bottom of the story the very paragraphs that I would have put at the top, had I been an unscrupulous, unethical journalist who cared for nothing but shock headlines to boost circulation. "That's where you get Monteith's speculation about dragons having been seen in Austin recently, together with a snapshot taken by those hippies whose *al fresco* pot party Adjdaak interrupted when he first came to this part of the world. It's a terrible picture, I don't think anybody would recognize it as a stooping dragon unless their imagination had been primed by the 'artist's conception' pictures earlier... huh, maybe that's why they put it at the end of the article, Monteith is setting the readers up to believe..." I swiped the screen to bring up the last paragraphs and said several words that my aunts think I don't know.

"Sienna?" Laura had turned away to flip the slices of French toast. "Why are you suddenly turning the kitchen air blue?"

I swallowed the last of my involuntary comments and stuck to the plain fact, which was quite bad enough without embroidery or profanity. "Somehow Monteith got hold of that awful snapshot of me, the one somebody took in Shorty's Bar just before I persuaded Adjdaak to get us out of there." Wild-haired and wild-eyed, the pale freckled woman in the picture did not look like anybody's idea of a sober, responsible head for an innovative language tutoring program. Monteith had given my name but, thank God, hadn't mentioned the business name. "Talk about bad publicity!"

"She does seem determined to tie you to the dragon sightings," Laura agreed as she dropped a fresh slice of French toast on my plate. "Not to mention your business, though at least she hasn't done that directly. Yet."

"Yeah. Let's *not* mention it. I probably won't *have* a business if anybody takes this *Grackle* nonsense seriously." And would that be such a terrible thing? I could go back to my old, lazy life of skating on the thin edge of financial ruin, and be left in peace. Was that too much to ask?

Evidently it was, because here came my nosy next-door neighbor, walking in the unlocked front door with a box of seedlings in her hands.

"Jenn! You're just in time for some French toast." Laura is better than I am at being nice to people.

"Oh, no." Jenn's long, ever so slightly horse-like face took on a superior expression. "I never ingest sugar, and I always get up with the sunrise, the way Nature intended. I had breakfast hours ago."

Granola and yoghurt, probably.

"I just stopped by to give you these," she said, thrusting the shallow box of dirt with green things sticking out of it at me. "Although I don't suppose you'll be wanting them now."

"Uh?" I can be more verbal than that, but this morning was taking it out of me already.

"Since you removed the rockery."

"The, ah?" Maybe I hadn't had enough coffee. I reached for the pot. Empty. "Where did it all go?" I muttered to myself.

"Yes," said Jenn, confusingly, "that's what I wondered too. It must have cost a bundle to pile all those rocks in your back yard. I was going to give you these cuttings to plant in the soil pockets. They're *scutellaria*."

Not a word in my Latin vocabulary.

"Texas rose," she translated. "They grow about six to twelve inches high, and they're drought-tolerant, so they're a responsible choice for a xeriscaped garden. And elves like them."

I refrained from rolling my eyes. Jenn's blend of eco-righteousness and cute whimsy could be hard to take. "They would have been perfect for little soil pockets in the rocks," she went on. "Why did you have the stones taken out again?"

Taken out again? Had Adjdaak disappeared during the night? Suddenly I realized what I *hadn't* been hearing all this time in the kitchen: those rhythmic, grating snores. I jumped up and ran through the tiny back porch, then caught my breath. No, he was there. Still doing his best impersonation of a vaguely dragon-shaped pile of silvery gray rocks. Although now that I looked closely, he wasn't in quite the same position he'd assumed during his day of digesting. Now he looked more like a pile of rocks that had been plopped down at random, with one rear leg splayed out in an impressive display of talons like crystal spears. And... were those loose scales that I saw scattered on the porch steps? I picked one up: fan-shaped, flexible, dark, and I was pretty sure that if I took it into a dark enough room I'd be able to see a shimmer of electric blue light along the edges.

"Oh," said Jenn, behind me, "I see. You know, I could have sworn that when I got up this morning the rocks were all gone, but I guess you were just rearranging them." She squinted uncertainly at Adjdaak's prone shape. "I don't want to be *critical*, dear, but I do believe I liked the previous arrangement better. And don't you think those clusters of long quartz points are a bit too New Age?"

"Maybe the quartz is too prominent," I agreed. "I hope I can get it back to the original arrangement."

Jenn was staring at my hands now. "What kind of lotion do you use?"

"Huh?" I had definitely not had enough coffee for this conversation.

"Gardening is so hard on my hands. How did you arrange all those rocks without even chipping your manicure?"

"Uh… really good gloves? And, um, it's a gel manicure. More expensive, but it dries super-fast under UV light and then it's guaranteed for a month." That part, at least, was true. In the run-up to starting the business, Floss and Blossom had convinced me that getting a guaranteed long-lasting manicure monthly would be less trouble than doing my own nails and constantly making repairs where the polish chipped.

"Oh. I don't use chemicals on my nails, of course. But it *is* so difficult, because gardening makes my hands too rough to gather fine fabrics…"

When she wasn't looking at my house through her kitchen window, or puttering in the garden, Jenn did crafts stuff. Mainly she made cloth dolls, fantastic long-fingered elves and fairies costumed in scraps of silk that she had, of course, dyed herself with vegetable dyes. The loose-limbed, big-eyed creations were actually quite lovely, with their languid, graceful poses and their costumes in woodland hues. I had a vague idea that I might want to buy one some day, but I'd never quite steeled myself to meeting her prices. She did her own photography; the dolls appeared in glossy fashion and craft magazines, and no matter how often she raised her prices she never had any extras to sell locally.

Jenn dithered on for a while about the difficulty of handling silk habotai, the need for specialty tools like curved needles for face sculpting and hemostats to turn the dolls' fingers inside out, her favorite kinds of moss and lichen, and where the seedlings she'd brought should be placed. Eventually she talked herself into the reasonable position that they could hardly be planted until I'd come to a final arrangement of the rocks making up the basis of the garden. After a bit more dithering about climate zones and growing seasons, she finally abandoned the tray of seedlings on top of the dryer and wandered back to her own house.

"Adjdaak, are you all right?" I demanded once she was safely out of earshot. "Where did you go? Are you hurt?" Those loose scales worried me.

One saucer-sized topaz eye slid open. "I am deeply wounded," Adjdaak announced.

"What? Where? What happened?"

"Do not gabble like that other human," he reproved me. "It is my *feelings* that are wounded. To think that my own worshippers would turn on me so viciously!"

Laura and I were both appalled by his story, although in different ways. Laura was appalled that anybody would be so evil as to shoot Adjdaak. Primed by Michael's story about the shotgun-toting farmer protecting his sheep, I wasn't terribly surprised by that bit. But I was dismayed to find that Adjdaak had fallen for such an obvious trap.

"Adjdaak, didn't it even occur to you that a goat tethered on a hilltop was bait for a trap?"

His eye began to close. "Why would it be a trap? That is how my people customarily make their offerings. Besides, there was vodka."

The people who'd shot at Michael in Nebraska? Could they have tracked Adjdaak here? And why vodka? "Were they Russians?"

The eyelid slid up slightly. "I like Russians. The Taklans never think to offer me vodka, but Colonel Grisha always brings some."

"Yes, but, but… Adjdaak, these Russians are bad men. They tried to kill Michael in Nebraska, and now they're trying to kill you!"

"They are not trying very well. All their weapons accomplished was to loosen a few scales that would have fallen off in the warm season anyway. Go away. I want to enjoy digesting my goat *á la Russe*."

Clearly Adjdaak was not going to be open to intelligent planning until he was less stuffed with goat and vodka. I wondered if planting Texas rose seedlings in all his crevices would persuade him to stay where he was. Didn't seem likely.

Laura had gone back inside while I talked with Adjdaak. She had come a long way since her first sighting of the dragon, but she still regarded him as something to be regarded warily, from a distance, rather than as a large foreigner who kept getting himself in trouble. No doubt that was a less stressful view of the dragon business; too bad I couldn't adopt it.

Now the raised voices coming from the house warned me that the kitchen might not be all that low-stress just now. "And *stay* there!" Laura shouted, punctuating the advice with a crash that somehow managed to sound both shattering and sticky.

I tiptoed through the back porch, past the washer and dryer, and peeked into the kitchen. It seemed to be empty now, but there was a spatter of French toast on the far wall, dripping syrup down onto the broken remnants of the plate. And now Laura appeared to be yelling at someone in her bedroom. I grabbed the frying pan in case she needed help.

By the time I got out of the kitchen, though, I realized that Laura didn't need any help. Not the kind that involved bouncing a frying pan off somebody's skull, anyway. The shouting and screaming was interrupted by sobs, and a man's low, calm voice overrode the hysteria.

Duke.

How had he gotten out of jail so fast?

I could only hope that he'd made a mistake by hot-footing it back to Austin, that Laura was still angry enough not to make the mistake of taking him back. She could do *so much* better for herself! I'd been thinking that for the two years she'd been involved with Duke, though I'd never made the mistake of saying it. But I had cheered inwardly when she came back from tour vowing never to let Duke into her life again. That man was Laura's weak point, much as that jerk Craig had been mine before Floss and Blossom, of all people, had made me see how worthless he was.

Craig... I shivered as if somebody had walked over my grave. When I did break up with him, he hadn't left nicely. He'd lost his temper and berated me and threatened me until I was ready to get my Smith & Wesson out of the safe and evict him at gunpoint. I really ought to stick around in case Laura needed help evicting Duke. That was now; Craig was, thank God, history. More than six months past and never a peep out of him.

From the changing sounds in Laura's rooms, though, I was very afraid that her "now" was also history, at least as far as the optimal moment for getting

Duke out of her life went. She'd quit throwing things and was beginning to interrupt Duke's low-voiced, incomprehensible speeches with an occasional watery chuckle. When I'd eavesdropped long enough to feel sure that reconciliation was, dammit, next on the menu, I left them to it. True friends didn't listen in on one anothers' love lives. Especially if your friend's choice of man left you a little bit sick to your stomach.

Anyway, they had all day to play at breaking up and making up. I had another seven and a half hours of tutoring sessions ahead, and then I really needed to make some changes so that I didn't keep getting into the bind of having too much business to take care of the business. And before all that, I needed to get Rukshana up and see that she ate something. Always assuming she'd gotten over last night's quarrel.

17. The best-laid plans

It took Bogdan quite a while to convince the boss of their need for serious armaments. Getting them into the country and procuring a couple of scoped rifles, the boss said, had been quite enough trouble what with all the ridiculous laws the Americans made about who could buy what guns where.

Bogdan mentally discounted that complaint; he figured the boss had enough contacts among his American counterparts that evading gun control laws was the least of his problems.

"And how do you know you need something better?" the boss demanded next. "You never asked for any weapons but rifles before."

"In the Pamirs," Bogdan pointed out, "we were tasked with capturing a dragon, not with killing one."

"And you never succeeded."

True, as far as it went, but hardly fair. "And I needed more people, and fireproof nets and ropes, none of which you supplied. We've never had the support we needed. As for now – killing may be easier than capturing, but this is the first time we've shot a dragon. How were we to know what was needed? The rifle rounds just bounced off its scales, and one of the rifles exploded when the thing breathed fire on it. We need better weapons. If you're serious about killing and destroying this dragon before the Americans capture it, you'll get us some."

Then he had to endure a tongue-lashing for "carelessly" losing one of the rifles and, worse, one of his subordinates. Bogdan was thankful that the "medic" he'd found for Zhenya's burns had come through with an entire botle

111

of fat white pills that not only assuaged the pain of the burns but sent Zhenya off into some kind of wonderland where he lay tunelessly humming to himself and chuckling at intervals. It wouldn't have done much for his control of the mission if Zhenya had been in any shape to understand how the boss was berating Bogdan. Nor would Zhenya quite have understood Bogdan's explanation that after the dragon's fire caused the rifle to explode in his hands, Kostya had been mortally wounded so that the only thing to be done was to put him out of his suffering. It was true enough from Bogdan's point of view: an underling with a shattered hand would be useless to the mission as well as posing a danger to them all, so from the moment of his injury Kostya was already as good as dead. Zhenya, though, was soft enough to have thought Kostya could have been saved. Better not to have that discussion.

"I trust you policed your brass!" the boss wound up after, reluctantly, accepting the necessity of deleting Kostya and agreeing that it was worth investing in better weapons rather than risking American control of a dragon.

"Of course," lied Bogdan, while a nasty little chill found its way to the back of his neck. It hadn't even occurred to him to look for the casing ejected from the Tokarev, let alone those from the rifles. He'd had more than enough to worry about, what with concealing the body, picking up that scattering of dragon scales, and putting off the gabbling peasant who'd arrived too soon at the scene and what was worse, kept waving his camera around.

Oh well, the ejected brass was hardly likely to be a problem. Bogdan had watched five seasons of "Hawaii 5-0" dubbed in Russian, enough to give him a thorough understanding of how American police operated. They always yelled at suspects, identifying themselves, while those suspects were far enough away to run from them. They spattered crowded downtown areas with lead and never asked where all the bullets had gone, probably for fear they'd learn how many innocent bystanders they'd winged or even killed. They didn't bother to dispose of the corpses they left behind. What were the chances they'd be meticulous about somebody else's shell casings? And their minds were more on their sex lives than on the case they were supposed to be working...

Bogdan sighed a little, very quietly. *Why* did American cops have such excellent sex lives? Russian women were more sensible, they wanted nothing to do with official or unofficial police. Which was laudable, of course, but occasionally Bogdan dreamed of being an American cop, of living in a fine house in a tropical paradise and constantly meeting beautiful women who found his occupation an aphrodisiac.

"Pay attention, *gopiets!*" the boss snapped.

Bogdan exited his brief daydream and paid very close attention to the instructions for picking up the improved ordnance he'd requested. It take some time to procure, and the pickup would not be easy. "The Paso is far from Austin," he protested. "Texas is a very large *oblast.*"

"It is *El* Paso, not *The* Paso," the boss corrected him crisply.

"Does it not mean the same thing?"

"Not to those stupid Americans. If you call it The Paso they will not know what – oh, never mind. You will not talk to anybody, so the name of the city does not matter. You will procure a map – you *are* competent to buy a map, are you not? I will contact you again when it is time to drive there for the pickup. Now listen closely, here is how to find the man you must meet –"

The instructions were complicated, and the boss did not want him to write them down. He made Bogdan repeat them three times until he was sure all the details were correct. Bogdan did gather, during the repetitions, that he had to go to El Paso because it was on the border where this *oblast* of Texas met Mexico, and the weapon he had requested was easier to buy in Mexico than in Texas. He also read between the lines of the instructions: the man they were to meet was someone important in the Juarez cartel – who better to arrange the smuggling of an extremely illegal weapon? – and it would be extremely unwise for Bogdan to annoy him in any way.

"We don' need a map," Zhenya slurred when he began to come out of his drug-fueled euphoric haze. "GPS in car."

Maybe this drug kingpin would be able to supply him with more Oxycodone as well as the arms he had demanded. Life was much more peaceful with Zhenya relaxed to the point of incoherence. Bogdan did just allow the thought to flit across his mind that life would be even more peaceful with Zhenya permanently silenced; then he banished it. Somebody was going to have to meet the Juarez drug lord and receive the weapon, and Bogdan saw no need for his face to appear in that transaction. He'd have to cut down on Zhenya's drugs a few hours before the meeting so that he'd be competent for it. Then, there was no telling how and when they'd be able to lure the dragon back within range of their new weapon; there might be more people around than there had been that morning. Any search for the shooter would be vastly shortened if they found the body of a foreigner who'd committed suicide next to the abandoned missile.

***

Craig didn't like squinting at an iPad screen; he preferred to read a real newspaper while he was waking up in the morning. His current girl friend was, at least, trainable. She knew to have the *Austin American-Statesman*, a fresh pot of coffee, and – on the days when it was published – the *Austin Grackle* ready and waiting for him. He'd only had to slap her around once, no more than a couple of love taps really, to make the point that he expected to find the newspapers crisp and untouched. She would have all the rest of the day to read through them and clip recipes, or whatever she did, after he was finished.

Thus, she had no idea why he snorted in disbelief at the discovery that the *Grackle* was wasting its front-page space on a fantasy story about dragons. Ridiculous – nobody could take this seriously – but he had to admit, it was also entertaining in a sick, twisted way. He finished his first cup of coffee while the top of his mind was reading about dragon mating rituals in some mountain range called the Pamirs, and while the rest of his mind was wondering if the Fern Monteith whose byline graced the article really believed what she had written. A pretty girl who would believe anything could always be amusing company... although there didn't seem to be a picture of the Monteith woman accompanying the article, so she was probably a dog. He flipped the pages of the journal, looking for the rest of the story, and stopped dead when he found the last page.

The second cup of coffee cooled while he studied that final paragraph and the picture accompanying it. He didn't waste mental energy on the speculation that a dragon had been seen in Austin, nor on the hopelessly blurred snapshot that was supposed to back up that speculation. All his attention was on the picture at the very end of the article, the crazy-looking female that the *Grackle* was trying, without much evidence, to tie in to the dragon story.

He stuck out his cup for a refill.

"Want me to pour the cold coffee out?" his girl friend asked.

"No, I want you to pour the fresh coffee on top so it splashes all over the table," he said with heavy sarcasm, and returned to studying that picture while she fussed about mixing exactly the right proportion of fresh, hot coffee, heavy cream, and one teaspoon of natural fructose. Well, well, well! He'd know *that* face anywhere. Sienna Brown! From the looks of it, she hadn't been doing all that well since she made the mistake of letting him get away. (He mentally skipped over the unpleasant details of what had actually happened; it just couldn't be that in a rightly ordered universe a woman like that, no longer young and never really pretty, could tell a stud like him to get out of her life. Hence, it hadn't happened that way – and he could tell from her distraught look in the picture that she'd had plenty of time to regret her mistake.)

The back page of the *Grackle* held another nasty surprise. The top right quadrant was filled by an ad for something called Sienna Language Services, and yes, it was *that* Sienna again: there was another picture of her, a much better looking one. For this photo she'd actually bothered to tame her frizzy reddish-brown hair into a sleek frame around her face. Not only that, but she was wearing makeup; the freckles were diminished, her mouth looked delectably large and full and there must have been a ton of eye makeup to make her eyes look so large and dark. He felt a reminiscent twinge. The first time he'd met Sienna had been at a party where she looked just like that, enticing enough to be worth his time. In the subsequent weeks he'd discovered that she didn't bother with makeup nearly often enough and that she wasn't nearly as grateful for his attention as a basically plain, tall, gawky woman should have been. Which was, after all, why he'd eventually stomped off after berating her for being a waste of time. (The details of the actual breakup were now comfortably buried under his preferred way of remembering the scene.)

If she'd been willing to take that much trouble with her looks on a regular basis he might have invested a few more weeks in persuading her to put out. But – she hadn't been, and he'd dropped the pointless pursuit, and why even think about it now?

Because she wouldn't leave him alone, popping out of the pages of his morning read with stories about for-God-sake *dragons* and ads for some kind of service she was offering now – and not the kind that had leapt to his mind when he first saw that glamour shot in the ad; when he read the fine print, she seemed to be offering some kind of tutoring service. He remembered now that she'd occasionally been so rude as to turn down his offer to come over because she had to tutor some stupid girls who were on the verge of flunking Spanish – what had their names been? Candyfloss and Bosomy? Something like that. And each of them was miles better looking than Sienna, and they doubled the effect by being identical twins. He should have carried them off with him under Sienna's nose, *that* would have shown her what a real man wanted.

That niggling urge to show her what was what started bothering him again. He sat reading the ad over and over while Ashley cleared away the breakfast things, fixed her face and finally trailed out the door to go to her job, looking wistful because Craig hadn't kissed her good-bye this morning. This tutoring service had an address right there on the Drag. Wouldn't it surprise Sienna if he just dropped in while she was sitting there, all lonely and waiting for some idiots to pay good money for her services! He could intimate, without actually promising anything, that enough time had passed he was willing to let bygones be bygones. She'd probably jump at the chance to have a real man in her life again. And then, as soon as she started counting on him to take her around and show her a good time, he could drop her – *hard*, and without warning, the way she'd....

His mind skittered around that humiliating breakup scene. Resolutely, he pushed that out of his memory and concentrated on the pleasure it would be to let Sienna know what it felt like to be dumped for no reason...

Or not. Depending on how cooperative she was willing to be. The previous fiasco might have taught her that she couldn't get away with taking that high and mighty tone with everybody. Lots of men wouldn't have been willing to overlook her freckles and her frizzy hair; maybe she'd learned that by now. He'd always felt Sienna had the ability to be real sweet, if she ever got over her high opinion of herself. If she was humble enough, grateful enough for his attentions, maybe he wouldn't dump her. That house of hers was a lot more comfortable place to live than this dump of an apartment...

Presently Craig left the apartment and drove towards campus. He even made the sacrifice of paying through the nose for a parking place just three blocks from SLS's address on the Drag. Not sacrifice, he told himself; *investment.*

18. The dragon in my back yard, part 2

The small square room at the front of Sienna Language Services looked deadly dull to Rukshana this morning. For a day or two it had been fun to sit in a foreign-style chair behind a table with a glass top, to poke the buttons on the wonderful machine that Sienna called a *cell*, to direct callers back to Sienna's office or get them to give her the magic code that would allow Sienna to speak with them herself when she was free. But the novelty had worn off all these experiences by yesterday afternoon, and the first rush of people wanting to sign up for tutoring had slowed, and she did not really understand why Americans liked to spend so much time staring at their *cells* and poking buttons to change the tiny, bright pictures on the screen. One of the nice boys who'd followed her back to the office the other day had shown her a game that he found fascinating, something about irritated birds. Rukshana had spent enough growing seasons in the fields, as a child, running and shouting and throwing stones to scare the birds away from the crops. *That* had been challenging – and sometimes a well-aimed stone brought down a bird and the children could bake it inside a mud casing, right there in the field, for a delicious snack.

But she was no longer ten years old, to run around bare-legged throwing stones and nibbling on bits of roast bird and raw grain. And playing with *artificial* angry birds, nothing but flat pictures sliding across the screen, seemed to her entirely pointless.

She wished somebody would come into the office and talk to her. Everybody she knew here in America seemed to be busy today. Just like yesterday, Sienna had disappeared into one of the small rooms in back, only coming out for quick breaks between tutoring clients in strange languages – *Ferenchi, Gairmani, Espani* – the only one Rukshana even recognized was *Rus*, and she hardly recognized that one the way the Americans pronounced it.

As for Sienna's man Michael, he was downtown today, whatever that meant, meeting with officials from the city to make sure all the requirements for the new business had been met; Rukshana vaguely imagined a group of elders like the Shaimak village council, standing around Michael in their long robes and embroidered hats and talking about... well, probably not about the last harvest and where to graze the sheep, but something equally dull.

Even Adjdaak, whom she'd expected to be her best friend and companion here in America, was selfishly concentrating on the handful of scales he'd somehow lost early this morning, probably by doing something stupid which she could have advised him against if he'd bothered to let her in on his plans.

It had been fun, yesterday, talking to the nice woman who called herself a reporter, whatever that meant. The woman who asked so many silly questions and had so much trouble understanding plain, straightforward answers. Rukshana giggled to herself, remembering some of the confusion the woman had shown over simple matters like Adjdaak's mate and the typical dragon arrangement for child-rearing, where the female laid the eggs in the male's nest and he spent a hungry winter keeping them warm until they hatched. She wouldn't mind seeing the reporter again today...

But Sienna would be angry. Rukshana's cheeks grew warm as she remembered how negative, how downright *insulting* Sienna had been last night! After the way they'd worked together in Shaimak to get rid of Sienna's enemy, she had thought the older woman was her friend, almost a sister – but just like everybody else, she got irritated and talked to Rukshana as though she was a little girl who had to be told to plait her hair and clean her nails! America was just as bad as the village: nobody understood that she was practically a grown woman, husband-ripe and ready to make babies of her own.

Rukshana sniffled, enjoying a moment of deep, dark gloom and self-pity. And then *he* came into the office. Rukshana's eyes widened. Tousled blond hair; stubble on the cheeks showing that he was a real man; muscles; the face of an angel.

"What language do you study?" she asked, opening the metal box called a *laptop* even though it sat on the glass desk top. She kept her eyes on the bewildering array of letters and symbols covering the bottom inside of the *laptop*, even though she had no idea what to do with them, because that Sienna would probably yell at her again if she caught her talking with a client about anything but work. And this particular client…! Rukshana stole a glance over the top of the *laptop*. Yes, definitely yummy. If she had not already vowed her heart to Rustam she would certainly be able to find things to say to this tall man with his long legs, his casual slouch, his lopsided sunny smile.

"Oh, I don't know," the stranger said. "What would you recommend?"

He sounded like one of those foolish boys who had followed her back here on that first day. Except that this was a man, not a boy, and his deep voice gave Rukshana a very enjoyable thrill deep inside. She raised her eyes again, met his gray eyes and that sweet, sweet smile, and forgot all about Rustam.

After all, if he really cared, Rustam would have come for her by now.

***

The top of Mount Bonnell was circled with yellow crime-scene tape for a full day while the Austin Police Department investigated the scene and collected what little evidence was to be found. There wasn't much, and what they did find raised more questions than it answered.

"What do you mean, the smudges on the rocks held trace elements of protein and alcohol?"

"Whatever happened, it wasn't just some kids starting a campfire," the forensics guy said wearily. "And it wasn't a lightning strike either. *Something* got burned up in that fire. From the strands of hair caught in the juniper branches, I'm guessing a goat. And a bottle of booze; in the crevices of the rocks there were some freshly broken pieces of glass. Consistent with a bottle of New Amsterdam vodka."

The lieutenant wrinkled his nose. He hated cheap vodka, and there was more and more of it on the street these days. "Peach or coconut flavor?"

"Not enough traces to tell. But it's looking like a cult sacrifice, wouldn't you say?"

"Santeria? But the corpse isn't —"

"I suppose," said Detective Martinez, "there's no actual law against middle-aged white guys following Santeria."

"Yeah, but *Russian* white guys?"

"Who said Russian?"

"Ballistics. The cartridge we picked up matched the bullet in the corpse's head. A 7.62 x .25 caliber. That's consistent with a Tokarev... an old one at that."

"I'm sure that caliber can be imported."

"Yeah, but who'd bother?"

All the same, the lieutenant found it easier to believe in an American with an antique Tokarev who imported the ammo he needed than in the wholesale importation of a Russian killer with his own weapon and ammo. Trouble was, that left them exactly nowhere with the current mystery: an unidentified corpse with a shattered hand, a singed face and a bullet in his head. A corpse whose prints were not in any American data base.

And a whole slew of near-witnesses, none of whom had seen the fatal encounter but all of whom wanted to tell him about the *dragon* they'd seen stooping down on the hilltop just before the fire, the explosion, and the pistol shot.

Lieutenant Flores had told Martinez to collect contact information, drivers' license numbers and, later, license plates, just in case one of the witness statements turned out to indicate something other than excessive consumption of pot. And he had watched the departing cars moodily, wondering why so many of them were festooned with the injunction, "Keep Austin Weird." A town with Russian followers of Santeria and mass hallucinations of dragons in the sky was already plenty weird enough for him.

Now, finally alone in his office, he fanned out the other incongruous things they'd found on the hill. The dark shapes were flat, thin, fan-shaped, flexible and unlike anything he'd ever seen before. Loose pieces from some kind of fancy costume? No, there weren't any holes for someone to sew them onto a tunic or whatever, and the undersides showed no trace of adhesive. They lay on his desk, three cards from a mysterious deck, and he was almost sure that the apparent flickers of iridescence were just reflections from the fluorescent light overhead.

Except, of course, that the light itself did not flicker…

***

Not only had Rukshana cheered up by the middle of the day, she'd actually remembered to go out to Subway and get me something I could wolf down between the tutorial sessions on French Reading Comprehension (psychology) and Italian Reading Comprehension (art history, and so much for my blithe assumption that none of my wandering-in graduate students would want Italian.) Tonight I was *definitely* going to put out an emergency call for extra tutors in major European languages, not to mention juggling next week's schedule so that I didn't wind up tutoring any more fourteen-hour days without breaks. I would have made a start on it while polishing off the bag of potato chips that came with the sub sandwich, but Italian Reading Comprehension showed up exactly on time, so *basta*.

I broke one of my own rules by interrupting the Italian session when I heard Michael's voice in the front room. "Hey!" I called, and went to the door. "Can you do a couple of little fixes for me? We need more tutors for graduate reading classes – French, German, Russian mainly – and I need you to fix my tutoring schedule for next week so I don't have more than six sessions a day, with a break in the middle."

"The scheduling program is supposed to make sure of that automatically," he pointed out.

"Yes, well, we had such a rush of clients that I kind of temporarily overrode that feature. A mistake. Now I need you to *un*-override it. Please? And I gotta get back to my Italian student. Art history. Zero verbal memory. And *fuori come un balcone*."

Michael looked slightly dizzy. "Outside like a balcony?"

"Nuts," I translated, and got back to explaining to Ms. Art History that we might call it the fifteenth century but to Italians it was *quattrocento*, and I couldn't help it that this sounded like "four century" to her. Since the Italians generated a lot of art history in the fifteenth century, not to mention twelfth, thirteenth, fourteenth etc., a grasp of their *fuori come un balcone* names for centuries was indispensable for her.

Michael made the changes I'd asked for, then interrupted a German tutorial that was actually going quite smoothly to point out that if I wanted to hire more tutors, I needed to build some slack time into my own tutoring schedule so that I'd be able to interview them. My first response to this perfectly reasonable and foreseeable request was neither polite nor reasonable; fortunately, it was in Hungarian, so neither Michael nor the client knew what I'd actually said. I begged him to work with Rukshana to clear places in my schedule and set up interviews.

"Rukshana's not exactly…"

I leapt to the assumption that she'd returned to her sulky demeanor of that morning. Perhaps I had not been sufficiently appreciative of the chicken avocado sub sandwich. Or perhaps the moon had gone back into its Moody Teenager phase. "Well… do it without her, then?" After all, a receptionist who was fluent in Taklan and Dragon hadn't been part of my original business plan. I had only suggested involving Rukshana as a way to keep her happy, and I was beginning to feel that this goal might have been overly ambitious.

In any event, the day ended better than it had begun. Michael worked wonders by way of inserting extra hours into a schedule where clients were already packed like sardines, we all got out of the office on time, and Michael and I were cheerful enough to hold hands on the way home. Rukshana trailed seven to ten paces behind us, kicking pebbles down the sidewalk and inflicting unnecessary wear and tear on my navy blue Reeboks that she'd taken from Adjdaak for her own use. Oh well, his super-strength dragon-quality toenails had already gone through the fronts of the shoes. Now they would go well with artfully frayed jeans like the ones Rukshana was wearing… which hadn't been frayed back when they were mine. Another trip to Buffalo Exchange might be in order, to see that both my uninvited guests could dress themselves without raiding my closet. But when would I find the time?

Not tonight, anyway. After two days of running very hard just to stay in the same place, I wanted some quality time. Michael, and peace and quiet, and food that somebody else had cooked, and Michael, and…

Well, I got Michael and a meal, anyway. Rukshana sulked off to the front room as soon as we got in. After a quick check to make sure Adjdaak was still snoozing in the back yard, Michael ordered us an Italian feast and drew me down on the living room couch while we waited.

"Your muscles are solid knots," he told me, pushing me down prone and probing along my spine with gentle, insistent fingers. "You need to let the office go for a few hours. I'm prescribing a back rub, then some good wine with dinner." He had ordered Asti's seafood and saffron risotto with a side of roasted butternut squash: comfort food for a March evening that was veering from near-spring warmth during the day to dampness and a penetrating chill as darkness came over the city.

"You're too perfect," I told him. "Frightens me. You don't know me that well; I might not be able to live up to your standard."

He chuckled. "Well, I already know that you use Hungarian expletives when startled, that your hair expresses the state of your psyche by escaping any restraints, and that you're a trigger-happy lady with that Smith and Wesson you keep in the gun safe. If you haven't managed to run me off yet, what new revelations do you think will do it?"

I stretched, purred, and felt the spaces beween my vertebrae opening out under his fingers. "You forgot Cath Palug. In listing my failings." Laura and I had adopted that cat too late in his life, after his self-image as a feral tomcat was already fixed. Getting him fixed in the other way hadn't changed him, nor had regular milk and kibble, petting with the magic silicon grooming glove, or a constant supply of squeaky stuffed mice.

"First," he said, "that wasn't a complaints list, that was a list of how you spice up my life. Second, I never forget Cath Palug, but I don't blame you for him. He is – what did you call him when we were first introduced?"

"The great plague of the House of Sienna," I said. The original Cath Palug had been one of the three great plagues of Ynys Môn in northern Wales.

"A force of nature, in short. Like your pet dragon."

"Adjdaak… isn't my pet. He's a visitor." One with a personality rather like Cath Palug's, come to think of it, only magnified by scales, talons, flame breath, and a body like an aerial armored tank.

His hands moved up and down my spine, relaxing muscles I hadn't realized were tense. I let myself melt down over the couch cushions and just exist. Cath Palug showed up and butted his head against my dangling hand, and I skritched gently behind his good ear. I could hear Rukshana talking quietly from the room on the west side of the living room, and from the corresponding room on the east side there was a drifting, half-formed melody taking shape on Laura's little keyboard. It all sounded good. Rukshana wasn't crying or yelling. Duke must have gone away. And Laura only pulled out the keyboard and composed songs when she was feeling particularly happy and peaceful: that was how a woman with an explosive temper and a bad habit of throwing expensive shoes got to be known in Austin mainly as a very sweet singer.

The tune she was working on now added to the sense of peace and fulfillment that permeated the house. It wasn't quite something you could hum – not yet – but you could sort of feel it heading that way, along with the snatches of words that came drifting out of the room. Something about a garden wall and falling leaves, about love and fate and finding a true home…

Both the front bedrooms, the one on the west side where Rukshana was crashing and the one on the east side that Laura had redecorated as a sitting-room inspired by an English flower garden, opened directly into the living room; part of the original architect's decision to save on hall space. Rukshana's door remained closed while she chatted away, but Laura's opened now and she swayed gracefully out to join Michael and me. She was wrapped in her old blue kimono; her cheeks were flushed and there was a fullness about her eyelids that made her look sleepy and contented.

"Oh, hi," I said, brilliantly. "Ah – Duke left?"

"For now…" Laura hummed a few bars to herself. "He'll be back."

"Oh." Swallow the disappointment; it is *never* a good idea to dis your best friend's boyfriend. "You guys made it up, then?"

"Mm-hmm. I didn't understand him."

In between fits of abstracted humming, Laura explained the world as she now saw it. Duke hadn't *wanted* to get in a fight; those jerks at the Copper Coyote had been insulting her personally, not just the band's music, and no real man could be expected to stand still while his girl was being insulted.

"Really? What did they say?"

"I didn't hear them, and Duke says I shouldn't know words like that anyway. He's very protective of me. You just have to *understand* him, Sienna. You can't expect him to let things like that pass. He's kind of like a dragon, don't you think? I mean, flaming my enemies…"

He was also, Laura informed me in between humming snatches of song lyrics, going to give up cocaine. For love of her.

I chomped down hard on my tongue and just listened.

"The dead leaves fell and he called it fate," she half-sang, "*Where is my home?*"

I figured that the street address of our house wasn't the deeply meaningful answer she was looking for.

Michael introduced his own slightly troubling motif into this conversation. "Who's Rukshana talking to?"

"Who cares, as long as she keeps it down?" I wanted to get back to that golden state of liquid contentment that his massage had induced.

"…keep Austin weird," Laura sang, "Like the dragon that lives in my back yard? *This is my home.*"

"It's just that, you know, she doesn't *know* anybody here except you and Thalia. And today she was talking to some remarkably sleazy type in the front office."

"Hazards of a public business. I take it you got rid of him?"

"For now."

I was too busy being revolted by the next bit of Laura's song to worry about Rukshana just then.

"My love is the dragon, my love is the fire,

My love is all of my heart's desire,

He is my home."

What, Duke was the dragon in her back yard? Yeesh.

"I guess she's talking to Thalia, then." I was *much* more worried about Laura just then, but I couldn't very well express my feelings to Michael while she was standing right there. And then the food arrived, and I called to Rukshana to stop chatting with Thalia and give my phone back, and we all wound up in the kitchen eating risotto and drinking bubbly, chilled white Cava from Barcelona, and I didn't even notice that Rukshana's sleepy, satisfied expression was the mirror of Laura's.

Not then, anyway.

19. But Tolkien wrote fiction

The rest of the week passed in a blur of new students, fiddling with the website, and calling in more tutors for the major European languages that all the graduate students were cramming for their reading comprehension tests. By Friday afternoon I was so wiped out that even being interviewed live on K-TEX's mid-afternoon program "Around Campus" seemed like a break.

To begin with, anyway.

Once the introductory niceties were over, it went far too much like the *Grackle* interview. I wanted to talk about language universals and plug the new tutoring service I was offering; the fresh-faced undergraduate who was nominally in charge of the interview wanted to talk about dragons.

I meant to keep pushing to move the subject back to Sienna Language Services, but... well. I was *tired*. I very much did *not* want to discuss the growing problem the business faced, which was that there was no way I could tutor all the languages I'd intended to cover *and* give personal attention to all the other clients *and* guide the other tutors in how to use my method. For that matter, I didn't even have a decent description of the method; I was beginning to realize how much my tutoring success was based on intuition and how hard it was going to be to put that into a training manual.

These thoughts led to the understanding that I really had let Michael rush me into opening the business too soon, and that was something I absolutely did not want to discuss on live radio. I didn't even want to discuss it with him; it was my fault for letting him push the opening date forward. Fighting all of his good reasons had seemed like too much trouble at the time.

Up to now, avoiding trouble had been a pretty good life principle, or so I liked to believe. I saved myself a lot of work by not getting around to things. Now I was having to rethink my entire philosophy of life. The way of the Austin Slacker was not going to cut it if I meant to run a successful small business. And I for sure didn't want to run a *failing* small business.

All told, I had far too many subjects to avoid. So I let the little girl push me around instead of counting to three and thinking. (Austin Slacker reactions again, see?) And she was much more interested in picking my brains about dragon sightings than in hearing about word order and syntactic tags.

"I really do not know why everybody wants to ask me about mythical beings," I tried.

She brought up that picture from the bar fight.

Eek! *Uno, due, tre...* When in doubt, lie. "Somebody else," I said firmly. "There may be a passing resemblance to me. That girl could even be a distant relative for all I know; both my parents came from Central Texas and I've got relations scattered all over the Hill Country and South Texas, most of whom I've never even met. But seriously, just look at that picture. *I* do not appear in public looking like that." Even for this radio interview, I had tamed my hair with a small fortune's worth of grooming products.

"The freckles?" the blasted girl asked.

"Another point. I don't have freckles." At least, I was counting on the new foundation and powder that Floss and Blosom had recommended to keep them decently covered up. "You're looking for a true redhead, somebody with fair Irish skin. That's not me."

From her skeptical look, I had a feeling that the spattering of freckles over my cheekbones and the bridge of my nose were popping out through the new makeup. But at least she didn't challenge me; she moved on to other subjects, or so it seemed.

I really don't know how we got onto the topic of what a dragon language would sound like. Probably because I was too tired to stay on my guard and keep counting and thinking.

"In the first place," I said, "*if* there were such animals as dragons, there's no reason to suppose they would have language. Why would you expect them to? No real animals have languages like human ones; a handful of chirps and other one-note signals is about as far as they get."

"I thought they'd taught some chimpanzees to use sign language."

"They taught them to use some signs. There's a lot of debate about whether they were ever able to put those signs together in a way that used syntax to elaborate their meanings. Washoe and Nim Chimpsky..."

Oops, too much information. She was looking lost. "But dragons are supposed to be old and very wise," the girl said.

"Sure, if you believe everything you read. Didn't anybody ever tell you that Tolkien wrote fiction, not natural history?"

She looked wounded, and I felt guilty. That had come out harsher than I'd intended. And my aunts had indoctrinated me in the fine Southern art of never hurting anybody's feelings – at least not in a way they would recognize until maybe the middle of the subsequent week. That, not giving me time to make up a good lie, had been the origin of Aunt Georgia's count-to-three rule. My aunts had socialized me so successfully that I hadn't even been able to break up with that jerk Craig whom I had made the mistake of dating, pre-Michael, until Floss and Blossom coached me.

So I felt guilty, and went along with her more than I'd intended to, and wound up speculating on what a dragon's language would sound like, *if* there were dragons, *if* they had language.

At least, I hoped she thought it was pure speculation.

"To begin with," I said, "their voice boxes and the rest of their anatomy would probably be nothing like what human beings have, so you wouldn't expect their language to sound like anything you've ever heard before. They might – probably would – have phonemes that humans can't even pronounce."

That got us onto the subject of phonemes, and I was able to waste a bit of time talking about something I actually understood until the interviewer wrenched the conversation back to dragon speech.

"So, phonemes are basically consonants. Like what?"

That was totally wrong. My explanation had gone in one ear and out the other. I suffered a brief wave of crippling doubt about my ability to teach the basic concepts of all human languages, and slipped up again.

"That's not correct, but it is true that people have more trouble with consonants in foreign languages."

"What consonants would dragons have that we can't pronounce?" she demanded.

Nngwe, pedi, tharo. That initial "nng" sound, typical of Bantu languages, drives Americans crazy. "The whole point is that I'm human, so naturally I wouldn't be able to pronounce them for you." Unlike *nngwe,* which was comparatively simple.

"But what would they *sound* like?"

Trouble was – I actually knew that, and I was too tired, rattled, and guilty to make up something. "Like rocks being crushed, or tectonic plates grinding, or things melting in fire. Hypothetically," I tagged onto the end, but she ignored me.

"How would noises like that possibly make words?"

"Well… they might be words like *q!x.* Or *dzhla#m.* Or *m?n.*" I didn't spell them, naturally, so at least she didn't know about the symbols that the first linguist to record the language had used for the noises I'd suggested.

She sighed happily. "Sounds a lot like the language of Mordor, don't you think? *Ash nazg durbatulûk, ash nazg gimbatul, ash nazg thrakatulûk, agh burzum-ishi krimpatul,*" she recited in the worshipful tones of a True Believer. "One ring to rule them all, one ring to find them, one ring to bring them all and in the darkness bind them."

A ring like that would certainly appeal to Adjdaak. The Black Speech of Mordor didn't sound much like his language – too many vowels, for one thing, and English word order, and complex syntactic markers – but I took the out.

"You're right! That's probably where I got the idea, from reading, ah, uh…"

"*Lord of the Rings,*" she said. "Tolkien's master epic."

"Yeah. That's it. See, totally derivative."

But she got the last word.

"But wouldn't it be wonderful if there actually *were* dragons," she sighed, "and Austin had one of our very own? Talk about keeping Austin weird!"

I winced, because right now that popular bumper-sticker slogan reminded me of the song Laura had been working on. The one she was calling, "The Dragon in My Back Yard."

Fortunately we were out of time after that line, so I was able to make my escape. So much of the interview had been a blur of nervousness that I managed to believe I hadn't actually given up too much information. As for Austin having a dragon of its very own, that dragon was going straight back to Shaimak if I had anything to say about it, and then I wouldn't have to worry about dragons and rumors of dragons any more, *ever*.

Over the weekend Rukshana dug in her heels, refused to even talk about going home, and threw an impressive temper tantrum whenever I so much as mentioned the subject. And Adjdaak used her as an excuse to stick around, although I suspected in his case the attraction had more to do with cheeseburgers and pizza and a newly acquired taste for spicy buffalo wings. The greedy guy couldn't really be that much invested in furthering a sulky teenager's gesture of defiance!

Oh, well. It's not as though there was any *evidence* of a dragon in Austin. Just a bunch of rumors that would naturally die down as some other fad took over.

I was able to believe that until Monday morning, when half the new registrants came in demanding to learn the language of dragons.

Those demands continued all week, no matter how often or how firmly I turned people away. I had to add being the front-office receptionist to my other duties; I couldn't trust Rukshana not to talk, and anyway she seemed to have lost interest in the job. She said she was quite happy to stay home and watch TV – her latest discovery of American life. Friday came as a relief, or so I thought as I staggered home from another week of being severely overscheduled. I fell asleep over the dinner that Michael thoughtfully provided – cooking was not on my agenda that week – and so I didn't know about the new disaster until I met Laura in the kitchen at ten-thirty the next morning. That was late for me because I was totally exhausted, but it was early for her on the day after a singing gig. She was all bouncy and happy like a morning person, and it wasn't until the third cup of coffee that I grasped what she was so happy about.

"They liked it, they really liked it! I've even been approached about a recording contract. It's going to be a hit, Sienna! And of course I've been asked to sing for Dragonfest."

"Huh? Dragon*what*? What's going to be a hit?"

"My new song, 'The Dragon in My Back Yard.' I just *told* you, Sienna," she said reproachfully. "We debuted it last night at Songsmithing."

I didn't want to hear this, so I deflected into trivia. "Isn't that an unusual venue for you, a folksong coffee house?"

"Sienna, you don't understand anything about music. It's not *folksinging*," she said scornfully, "it's modern lyrical pop. Would you call Elsa's 'Let it Go' in *Frozen* a folksong?"

"I'm guessing the correct answer is no."

Laura threw up her hands. "I suppose it's no use trying to explain the difference."

"None," I agreed. I could just about carry a tune in a basket, but that was the limit of my musical ability. And it hadn't been a very good distraction; I was still worried. "What's Dragonfest? I've never heard of it."

"It's new – inspired by the dragon sightings around town lately. But I think it's going to be as big as Eeyore's Birthday Party," she explained, referencing an Austin institution that had grown from a beer party in a vacant lot to a mass beer-and-music daylong party that filled Lamar Park.

Oh, joy. Austin was developing a dragon cult. And my mission in life was sending their only actual dragon back to his home in Taklanistan.

Well, my secondary mission. My first one had to be revamping Sienna Language Services in line with my original goals. Didn't it?

I decided on Saturday that the business really had to be my first priority, because Adjdaak flatly refused to consider leaving Austin before the great festival in his honor. There was also, he reminded me, the problem of Rukshana's future to consider.

Oh, well. According to Laura, Dragonfest wasn't supposed to happen until the weekend after next. By then maybe I'd have solved all the other problems: Rukshana would understand that she couldn't stay here indefinitely, she and Adjdaak would go home, and Sienna Language Services would be back on track to becoming the innovative, wildly successful tutoring service I'd first envisioned.

Given that she had nothing even faintly resembling the proper papers, not even a passport, I had some hope that a little chat with a lawyer specializing in immigration issues would soften Rukshana's attitude. Especially if we mentioned Immigration and Customs Enforcement. True, Austin considered itself a sanctuary city, but I suspected the "sanctuary" part applied more to brown people from just over the border than to a blonde girl from thousands of miles away who had no explanation for her presence in America. Not that I was going to say that to anybody, being that it was probably a racist thought that could get me Twitter-mobbed and destroy my business in no time flat. But I could think it.

Aunt Georgia, being an Austin realtor, had a professional interest in knowing everybody in town. I managed to offload the search for an immigration lawyer to her without explaining precisely why I needed one – the second part was the hardest – and then, not before time, settled down to redesigning the business. I had a quiet day for it. Laura was rehearsing variations on the song and accompaniment with Duke's band, and I'd sent Rukshana off to the weekend crafts fair on the Drag with some money to buy some beaded earrings like those she'd been wistfully noticing on the hippie holdovers around campus. Hank had asked Michael to go to a UT conference on Mayan glyphs, which probably meant he was going to be headed for the Yucatan soon. And the March weather had turned chilly and grey again, so Adjdaak was probably going to continue his semi-hibernation as a rock garden in the back yard. I looked forward to a nice, quiet, undisturbed day to focus on how we would get back to something resembling the original business plan.

Like the business plan, that didn't work out anything like I'd expected.

20. Empty eyes

There were two of them, and they simply walked in through the unlocked front door. I had my head in the computer, so to speak, working on an Excel spreadsheet that Michael would later translate into a revised schedule, and for some reason – possibly because it was the problem that was giving me the most fits at the moment – I just glanced up and assumed they were foreign students interviewing for the German or Russian tutoring positions that had just opened up. Probably Russian, I thought. I don't know why. And I don't know why it didn't occur to me that none of the ads for tutors gave my home address; maybe because I'd been concentrating on work to such an extent that I felt like I was at the office. Anyway, all I said when I glanced over the top of the screen was, "Just a minute, I'm busy."

Intending to talk to them one at a time, *after* I'd saved the current mess that was supposed to become a proper spreadsheet.

Then the laptop went whirling off the table, I jumped up and yelled, and the one who hadn't thrown the laptop was behind me and had hold of my arms.

I filled my lungs again and the one in front of me moved around the table like lightning and hit me across the face, open-handed, so hard that my head rocked sideways and for a moment I thought my neck would break.

"Even think about screaming," he said, "and you'll get my fist instead of a little slap."

In a Russian accent.

Fury and hatred consumed me. I couldn't think. My cheek hurt so much

I wanted to put a hand up to see if anything was broken, but of course while I was thinking that the other one was tying my wrists behind my back. Felt like zip ties. More efficient than the duct tape Edward Osborne had used last fall.

Osborne was now a pile of bones at the bottom of a deep gorge running through the Pamir Mountains in Taklanistan, and I wished the same fate on these two goons. Maybe somewhere closer though. I didn't want to go to Taklanistan with them. For that matter, I didn't plan to go to the end of the street with them if I could help it.

I managed to tamp down my feelings and pretended to be reasonable instead. "If you want jobs as Russian tutors for my company, this is a really bad way to introduce yourselves. How about you untie me and we have a civilized conversation instead?"

"How did you know we were Russian?"

I tried to shrug. Not so easy with my hands tied behind me. I tried to stay hopeful; at least he was talking now, not hitting. And now that I wasn't half blinded with pain and hatred, I thought this one was young and slightly shaken up by his own violence. "Easy. Your accent. I am a professional, you know."

The one behind me, whom I hadn't properly seen, chuckled and said something in Russian. *It doesn't matter, Zhenya. Keep to the point.* His voice was cold. Strictly business. Could he be reasoned with?

I decided not to let them know that not only did I recognize the accent, I could understood everything they said to each other. It gave me a slight edge. Not enough to overcome two bastards who'd already tied me up and hit me, but all I had at the moment. Almost all. The other thing could cost me too much to use.

"Where is it?" the one behind me growled.

Adeen, dva, tre. As long as we were doing Russian. "Where's what?" My gun? Or did somebody else know the secret of the dragon's speech, and they were after the flash drive where the language data was stored? Either way, ignorance seemed my best chance. If they didn't know about the flash drive, so much the better. If they didn't know about the gun… Right now I didn't see much chance of getting to the gun safe, but maybe I could get them to untie me on the pretext of leading them to where "it" was.

This time it was a fist that crashed into my face instead of an open hand, and it hurt so much I whimpered involuntarily and tears sprung into my eyes. Oh, I'd grown too soft and felt too safe since Michael came into my life. Last year I'd never have been alone in the house, even on a quiet Saturday afternoon, without the Smith & Wesson loaded and close to my hand. Last year I'd have been standing and ready to shoot the moment somebody I didn't know broke into the house. (And they'd have had to break in, because last year I wouldn't have sat down to work in an empty house without checking the locks and windows first.)

"You know what we want."

I shook my head and regretted the motion. That hurt too.

The one behind me, the one with the cold, cold voice and the thicker accent, spoke again. "Where. Is. The. Dragon." Something cold stuck into my bruised face. Cold and round. I could guess what it was without seeing it, and I was so scared I damn near wet my pants. But not too scared to think, not yet.

Igui, igam, !nona. The "!" represents a click in Khoisan. "I'm sorry, dragons are mythical beings. Why don't you ask me for something that actually exists in this world?" I didn't want to tell them that Adjdaak was asleep in the back yard, his thoughts and reflexes sluggish in the chilly weather. That wasn't just me being heroic, in case you're wondering. I'm not a hero. I'm just reasonably bright, and I didn't give much for my chances of surviving once I'd given them what I wanted, unless they were stupid enough to tackle Adjdaak before they killed me. Couldn't count on that. And I'd already had a look at their faces.

This time I was braced for another blow, wincing in advance, but it didn't come. Instead there was a chuckle from behind me, and two hands on my shoulders pushing me down into the dining room chair where I'd been sitting while I worked. I really wished the unseen guy would come around where I could look into his eyes and maybe guess what he was thinking. That invisible chuckle chilled me to the bone.

Rough hands fastened my upper arms to the chair, using more zip ties, and he wasn't careful about how tight he pulled them. I wondered how long it would take before they cut off my circulation. Then I wondered if I was going to live long enough for that to be a problem.

And then he came around where I could see him, and I wished he hadn't. His face was like a stone carving – a rough one, unfinished – and his eyes…

His eyes were blue and cold. One was staring and blank; the other one was… worse, because it could see, and it wasn't seeing *me*. It was seeing a thing to be crushed. I couldn't restrain a shiver.

My great-grandfather claimed that he'd once met Pretty Boy Floyd, the outlaw. My great-grandfather was a giant of a man, six foot six even in old age. According to family lore and his own stories he'd been something of a brawler in his youth, and not given to backing down or admitting fear no matter what the odds against him. But he told me that he'd been afraid of Pretty Boy Floyd. "Don't believe that song about how he give poor families a Thanksgiving dinner," he'd warned me – unnecessarily; I'd never heard the song. "That boy was a stone killer. There wa'n't nothing behind his eyes, you get me? Blue and cold and empty as a March sky."

The description fit the man who'd tied me up. And I knew now, oh yes, I knew exactly why Great-Grandpa Jim had been scared. This man would kill the way I'd step on a cockroach, except he'd be less bothered about it afterward.

"You seem intelligent," he said softly, "for a woman. In fifteen minutes you will be begging me to let you tell what you know… and maybe I will stop what I am doing then, and maybe I will not. Why not save your pretty face and tell me now?"

There were tears in my eyes from the pain of the blows. But pain hadn't made me stupid or suicidal – not yet. I did have that one weapon that they didn't know about. I didn't want to use it, because it might kill me. But it would be better than being tortured to death.

He snapped a command to the younger man, the one called Zhenya. In Russian. *Go to the kitchen, find tools and prepare them.*

If I hadn't already been so scared that my face was drained of blood, I would have turned white then.

Will you bring her to the kitchen?

I might as well. The tools will cool down if you have to carry them back out here.

I closed my eyes as the big man dragged my chair over the sill and into the kitchen. I needed to concentrate. To get past the terror and the anticipation of pain, and activate my last hope, because I needed to do it right the first time.

We have a gas range. Immediate fire. Not a good thing, now. As soon as the chair legs thumped down on the floor I felt a hand on the side of my head, holding me still, and then a line of fire burned along the other side of my face. I shrieked and the big man clapped a hand over my mouth as he moved the burning thing away. I thought it was gone. It was hard to tell, my face hurt so much. He laughed happily, like someone who was having a wonderful time. "If we have to gag you, you will not be able to beg me for permission to talk. You would regret that."

When I made myself look through screwed-up, watering eyes, I saw that he was holding one of the shish kabob skewers from the junk drawer. With a hot pad wrapped around the end. Naturally. It must detract from the joy of torture if you get hurt at the same time you're inflicting agony on your victim.

He turned away to thrust the skewer back into the leaping flames of the front burner. My cheek throbbed as if it was still on fire. The pain made me feel sick at my stomach. "Next time," he said, "it will be your eye. I find that the loss of one eye vastly increases a subject's desire to preserve the other one. Which do you prefer to lose, the left or the right?"

My mouth was dry.

"Come now," he said, like someone encouraging a child to speak up. "The eye is lost anyway; perhaps I will give you a chance to tell me about the dragon afterwards. Now choose. Will you have the left eye or the right one burned out?"

I worked up enough saliva to say what I needed to say, and opened my mouth.

"*O!dm ynd?moq.*" It was not necessary to scream. New pain lanced through my forehead as I pronounced the words. The man with the skewer shouted and let it drop on the stove to beat at the flames coming out from under his clothes. But the other one wasn't bothered. What had I done wrong? Oh! Plural, dammit, plural! It came to me through the burning and the blinding pain in my forehead. "*Idz?ldm dzynd?moq! Idz?ldm dzynd?moq!*" I was shouting now, over the screams. My vision was blurring. No! I *had* to fight the side effects long enough to do this right. "*Idz?ldm dzynd?moq d'lq! Idz?ldm dzbezhd#ml!*" The men burn totally; the men are consumed. Yay for me, remembering plurals *and* the passive marker under stress, I thought as the pain took over my whole head and a merciful blackness engulfed me.

21. Rattlesnakes are natural

I was on my back. My cheek still hurt, but when I put up my hand I felt nothing but some kind of padding over it. Someone took my hand and moved it, and I wrenched it free. If they'd untied me, I was damned if I'd go passively.

My face was wet, where it didn't hurt. "Sienna, Sienna!" It might have been Michael calling me, except his voice didn't sound quite right. I opened my eyes slowly onto a blurred, bright world. The light in the ceiling lanced renewed pain through my head and I shut them again.

"It's too bright for her. Turn that light off!" Definitely Michael, and he was angry with somebody.

If Michael was here, everything was all right. My head was whirling with scraps of language and bursts of pain. I couldn't have explained how I felt so sure of Michael, but I relaxed anyway. He was holding my hand now, and the brilliant ceiling light was no longer trying to burn through my closed eyelids…

Burn. My *eyes!* A jolt of panic shot through me and I struggled to sit up.

"Not yet, Sienna." A hand, gentle, on my shoulder; a familiar voice. "You're hurt."

"My *eyes?*" I croaked.

"The light hurts them? Still?"

"No. Are they…" Words floated away from me. "*Ynd?bemoq?*"

"Don't use that language!" Michael snapped, his voice sharp with alarm.

Oh, okay. I reached inside my head for better words. All the languages in the world were floating around in lazy spirals, and I couldn't find the one I needed. *Find ich euch in Feur... Elle réchauffe le cœur et brule le corps... Fieri sentio... Tiger, tiger, burning bright...* That one! "My eyes... burned?"

"Good God Almighty," said a stranger's voice. "Is *that* what they threatened to do to her?" An unfamiliar touch on my arm. "It's all right, Miss Brown. You're not hurt, apart from that one burn on your face. You're safe now. Nobody in the hospital is going to hurt you."

I heard a change in his tone, as if he had turned away to talk to someone else. "She's going to have a spectacular shiner for a few days. But she got lucky with the burn; there's no eye involvement at all."

Involuntary tears leaked out of my uninvolved eyes. If I hadn't found the right words... *what if it hadn't worked?*

I was desperate enough to find English again. "The Russians. The Russians aren't here?"

"*Nobody* is going to be let in except hospital personnel and me and Laura," Michael said. "There's a cop outside your door. Although I think he's here more to find out what happened than to protect you."

It was so hard to concentrate; it would be easier to drift away on those swirling, spiraling lines of language. But I needed...

"What happened?" I managed to say.

"Maybe you can tell us, when you're better. Laura found you –"

"No, Jenn did," Laura corrected. So she was there, too? I peered through my eyelashes and saw her face. Blurry, like everything else. "She said you screamed, and then two men ran out the front door and threw themselves into a car and drove away, and she went in..."

"Brave. Should've called police."

"Nosy, *I* think, and for once it was a good thing. Though she had some crazy story about the men being on fire, and thinking there was a fire in the house and she had to put it out."

It took me too long to assimilate each scrap of information. "Men... on fire?"

"Well, you know Jenn. She wouldn't want to say she was so desperate to find out what was happening that she charged in without waiting."

"What did she find?"

"You, in the kitchen, tied to a chair and passed out. The front burner of the range on full blast. And…"

I could guess what she didn't want to say. I didn't actually want to hear it. What had happened would fuel too many nightmares already; I didn't need to think about what other kitchen utensils my tormentors had planned to use in their improvised torture session. I was never going to use those skewers again, they could go to Goodwill as soon as I got home… I forced myself to concentrate, to stop floating in and out of nightmare. To use language.

"They were alive, then. Too bad." So much for the power of the language – the little bit I knew, anyway. "Maybe Adjdaak will teach me a stronger sentence for next time."

"Did—" Laura paused and looked at a man in scrubs. "Did *you-know-who* set them on fire?"

"No," I said. "I did."

"*You used the Language?*" Michael's face went white.

"Better than being blinded…" And the swirling, swooping darkness took me again.

Next time I woke, my head was clear. The room was dark and Michael was asleep in a chair beside the bed. I looked at him with greedy, happy eyes. I might never have been able to see him again… If the Russians… That was too frightening; I didn't want to think about it. Nor did I want to think about the blurred vision and memory problems when I first came back to myself. Something like that *always* happened when a mere human being used that language. I'd known that going in, and I'd chosen to take the risk because I thought that whatever happened to me would be better than what the Russians had planned. But if I'd had time to remember how Edward Osborne had destroyed his own mind while he tried to kill us with words from the dragon… if I'd thought about him babbling like a toddler until he stepped off that cliff under the delusion that he could fly…

That hadn't happened to me, and I was profoundly grateful that I'd passed out before I could do that to myself. When I woke the first time, confused and blurry – without consciously thinking it, I'd been afraid that I would pay for this use of the dragons' language with permanent brain damage. But my mind seemed to be healing itself, just like before.

Michael's head fell forward and he startled awake. "Sienna?"

"Here. Awake. *Sane.*" My head still hurt, but not nearly as much as my face. Oh, I'd forgotten the burn. I might still be too damaged for all practical purposes. Would Michael want to stay with a mutilated woman? Would I want him to? If he did, would he stay out of love, or charity, or a sense of duty?

Questions too hard to face, right now. Instead I asked him to tell me how I got to the hospital.

"What happened to you?" he demanded in turn. "Two men – who? What did they do to you?"

I shook my head. I didn't want to talk about it yet. "Later. Tell me…"

He said that we owed a lot to Jenn. Not only had she rushed into the house and cut me free, but she'd done all the right things after that. Called EMS, called him, called Laura. Ran cool water over my face and then applied a soothing lotion.

"Though I'm not just entirely sure how 'right' that was," he said. "It was aloe vera and some herbal mixture of her own. Green. Smelly. And there she was telling me how it couldn't do any harm because all the ingredients were 'natural.'" He snorted. "What's wrong with that lady, anyway? Loco weed is natural. *Rattlesnakes* are natural."

"She didn't grow up in Texas. She's originally from back east somewhere – Virginia? North Carolina? She thinks Nature is her friend." That wasn't an illusion many native Texans cherished.

"East Coast? *Hurricanes* are natural," Michael grumbled before finishing his part of the story. There wasn't much more to it; he'd come straight from campus to find Jenn and me in the kitchen, hadn't waited for EMS; he put me in his car and broke speed limits all the way to Dell Seton Hospital downtown.

"Wouldn't Seton Medical Center or St. David's have been closer?"

"Woman, aren't you too shaken up to second-guess me?"

"Never."

"Dell Seton," he informed me, "has the best trauma center in Austin. It's the kind of thing people in my line of work notice." I assumed he meant his jobs for Hank Henderson, not his as-yet-unpaid position as part-time business manager for Sienna Language Services. "Anyway, Laura met me here, they treated you, they're keeping you overnight because of suspected concussion. *Did* anybody hit your head, do you remember? They couldn't find any lumps, but the CT scan showed minor brain swelling. Which went down rapidly, thank God."

"Probably a measurable effect of using the Language." I thought it over. "You know, that could give us some very useful information about the Language and how it affects humans. If we could get hold of one of those scanners I could run some tests..."

"You could *not*," said Michael. "If you ever risk yourself by using that language again I will kill you myself."

"Even if it's the only way to save my life?"

"Hmpf! Okay, in that case maybe I'll let you off. But don't push your luck."

The next day, I told my story to a detective while Michael held my hand so tightly it almost hurt. He was very interested in the mention of Russians. For some reason he wanted to know if either of the Russians had been carrying a Tokarev pistol.

"I'm sorry, I didn't see any gun," I told him. "It happened so fast, they didn't need one, they surprised me..." I started shaking again and Michael growled at the detective.

"Oh well, you probably wouldn't have been able to identify it in any case," the detective said easily, "I know how girls are about guns."

He didn't quite understand why Michael snorted at that.

He wanted to know why they had picked my home to invade. Was I *sure* I didn't know them?

"You heard the lady," Michael said.

After a random series of other questions the detective thought he had figured out that the invader were looking for drugs that they thought we were withholding from them. He warned both of us about the dangers of the drug business, we both told him it must have been a case of mistaken identity because neither one of us was inclined that way, and tempers became short. Finally he went away, having recommended that in future I keep my doors and windows locked.

I meant to do that. I also meant to have my .38 Special close by at all times, and to resume keeping it between the mattress and the box spring at night. But I didn't feel he really needed that information.

They got around to discharging me late that afternoon, and Laura brought clothes and drove me home; Michael was busy installing a state-of-the-art security system. I'd had a look at my face after they took the dressings off. It was – not encouraging. I've never been pretty, and a blazing red, raised weal running diagonally up my cheek was hardly an improvement. Nobody would be able to look at me without staring.

The discharging doctor's cheerful words about ointments and quick healing and, if all else failed, laser surgery didn't make me any happier. All that was guesswork about the future. What if I had to live forever with the way I looked *now*?

"That," Laura said, "is also guesswork."

True, but it didn't make me feel any better.

I'd assumed that SLS was closed in my absence, but it turned out I'd been overly pessimistic. Rukshana had spent Sunday contacting every tutor on my list and telling them what had happened to me, and an amazing number of them had pitched in to cover my absence. Gabriela Gehrig, my annoying but very competent Classics specialist, was temporarily running the office. Mira Martinez, a T.A. I'd gone to school with, had stepped in to cover the Spanish and Russian tutoring, and people I didn't even know were on the French, German and Italian sessions.

"And they'll all be delighted to see you come back," Laura told me.

"Huh. Nobody's going to be delighted to *see* me," I said sadly, gingerly feeling the puffy edges of my burn.

"Replacing Gabriela Gehrig? They will draw your chariot through the streets to the applause of the crowd."

Oh, well. If she put it that way…

I thought I was getting better. I *was* getting better. And wasn't it great to be out of the hospital and sleeping in my own bed again? With Michael beside me, holding me, infinitely reassuring?

It was better all the way until one a.m., when I woke up screaming. My face was on fire and I couldn't see and… I screamed until the lamp came on and I could see again. My bedroom. Cath Palug stalking up and down at the foot of the bed, not pleased with me. And Michael, not some Russian gangster, holding me in his arms and talking until the horrors faded.

"I'm sorry," I whispered. That was after Laura had come to the bedroom door and Michael told her to go back to sleep, everything was all right. "I thought… I dreamed… It *burned*, and I couldn't see anything…"

"Do you want a pain pill?"

"*No.*" I had to be able to, to concentrate. To use the Language again if they came back. I consciously, carefully, slowed my breathing. "I'm sorry I disturbed everyone. Let's just go back to sleep, okay?"

But as soon as the lights were off, I started shaking.

"Looks like we'll be sleeping with a lamp on for a while," Michael said. "So that every time you half wake up, you'll be able to see, you'll know for yourself that your eyes are all right."

"I keep thinking… what if they come back?"

"I'm here now," Michael said. "So, two things you need to get clear. First: if they want to come at you, they'll have to get through me."

I leaned my unburned cheek against his shoulder. "And second?" I asked after a few minutes.

"Huh?"

"You said, two things."

"Oh! Second, *nobody* gets through me. And I'm going to be right here with you until this is cleared up, Sienna. I don't want to crowd you, I'm not trying to move in permanently, but I'm not letting you stay alone right now."

"Trust me, I do not feel crowded." I felt – well, still shaky – but relieved. And every time I woke up after that, I only had to see my room in the lamplight and feel Michael beside me before I fell asleep again.

The next day, Laura enlisted Floss and Blossom in her Sienna Recovery Strategy. She kicked Michael out, telling him it was time for some girl talk and he could go take care of business; Adjdaak would be on guard in the living room until he got back.

When she ushered the twin blondes into my bedroom I winced. It was hard to see even one perfect face right now. Two identical ones were two too many.

"Laura says you're worried about scarring." Floss hadn't heard of introducing painful subjects tactfully.

"Second-degree burns *are* likely to scar, but we know all about how to fix your face." Neither had Blossom.

"So far, you've done all the right things, but you need to be careful while you're healing. By Sunday it'll be healed enough for you to start working on not letting a scar form."

There followed an intensive session about such things as gently stretching the skin around the wound, applying aloe vera gel with Vitamin E, and keeping the area covered with sunscreen.

I was supposed to eat a diet rich in antioxidants and stay hydrated; they'd even brought me a special bottle of water marked off in segments to help me keep track of how much water I was drinking through the day.

For now, they'd brought me a special combination antibiotic cream/concealer recommended by dermatologists. And once everything was thoroughly healed, if I was still unhappy with my appearance, they assured me that they were personally acquainted with the best laser surgeon dermatologist in Texas.

"How come?" I asked. I couldn't quite imagine either of these sweet airheads dating a surgeon.

"Boob jobs," they said simultaneously.

"And not a scar to be seen," Floss assured me.

"Want to see?" Blossom offered.

"Um, I'll pass."

How about that? I'd always assumed their perfect figures were a gift from God, along with their perfect faces.

"Implants?" I surmised.

"Reduction," said Blossom.

DRAGON SCALES

"High school was hell," Floss volunteered.

"People think if you're, you know, built that way, you're easy."

"All the boys made bets about getting to, you know, *touch* us."

"I can imagine," I said. My particular high school hell had been pretty much the opposite: I reached my current height of 5'9" in ninth grade and didn't develop much otherwise until my senior year, by which time the "Sienna is really a boy" jokes were entrenched in Beeville High culture. But at least I hadn't had to deal with people trying to feel me up, which must have been even worse. The things I didn't know about my students... I changed the subject.

"You know, you two are really knowledgeable about skin care. Did you ever think about working as assistants to a dermatologist instead of getting education degrees?"

They looked at each other. "*More* classes?"

"No foreign language requirement, no Math 101," I said. "And I'm sure your father would be happy to pay for the training rather than..." *throwing away his money trying to force you to get university degrees...* "rather than more college tuition," I finished.

They promised to think about it, and I promised to follow all their instructions and stay out of the sun.

"That includes Barton Springs and the beach," Floss emphasized.

"You can stand to get through one summer without swimming."

Maybe.

Actually, if the business stayed this healthy, I'd be indoors under fluorescent lights all summer.

If people weren't totally turned off by my face.

"*Don't worry*," Floss said. "I can tell you're worrying, Sienna, your face just got all tense and you've got that little line between your eyebrows."

"Just relax and listen to a soothing tape," Blossom advised. "Sounds of the sea... well, maybe not that. I've got lots of meditation music on my phone; I'll download some tracks right now."

They were genuinely sweet girls, and they deserved a better future than working as primary-school teachers, a profession in which they had absolutely

149

no interest, just because an education degree was a good way to avoid intellectually challenging course requirements. I hoped they'd look into training for dermatology. Who knew, perhaps dating a surgeon wasn't impossible after all; there must be men out there whose main requirements for a wife were a sweet nature and a pretty face.

Lucky for me that Michael wasn't one of them.

I thought.

I hoped.

Then Blossom set up my phone to play Sounds of the Forest, and I stopped thinking and drifted off to sleep.

22. An amoral eavesdropper

The very next day I ignored all Floss and Blossom's recommendations and went charging off without even applying the magical concealer. In my defense, I had a very good reason for doing so.

Michael had gone to the office and Adjdaak had asked me if it was okay for him to take a short break from guard duty in the living room; he wanted to stretch out as a full-sized dragon for a few minutes. He promised not to go to sleep, and he hadn't: minutes later he came crashing into my bedroom. In order to fit into the house, of course, he'd had to change right back to human form. Being in a hurry, he hadn't stopped to grab the clean clothes I'd hung up in the laundry room.

It was all right. Sort of. I mean, I'd got kind of used to glimpsing a naked Adjdaak in the house. Although having him in my bedroom, when I was in bed, was a step too far. And I wasn't at all sure how Michael, who was leaving as much as possible of the business in Gabriela Gehrig's hands so he could spend time with me, would react if he walked into this kind of tête-à-tête.

"Adjdaak," I said as firmly as I could manage from my pillows, "go back to the laundry room and put on your pants. *Right now.*"

"No time," he said. "Rukshana... she..."

In his agitation he switched into Taklan, speaking very fast, and I wasn't sure I got all the details. But what I did get was bad enough.

Rukshana wasn't at the house or the office. She'd gone somewhere else, with a man Adjdaak didn't know, and he wasn't letting her leave. She was terrified, and she'd called out to Adjdaak in the language of the dragon, and no, he wasn't sure how much using the Language had hurt her; he wasn't getting anything from her now but a sense of fear and pain.

I was out of bed and dressed before he finished. "Can you find her?"

He hesitated. "I can smell her out… in dragon form. In this form, I am not sure."

A good thing he hadn't wasted time getting dressed, then.

We headed out to the back yard and he changed form in the blink of an eye – the first time I'd seen the transformation, and I was impressed. I wondered how he got around the conservation of mass and energy, and I hoped Jenn hadn't been spying on us from her kitchen window, but both these thoughts only passed through the back of my mind. He lowered his neck and I scrambled onto his back and took hold of the lowest of the projecting neck spines. *Should have grabbed my jeans instead of a skirt, good thing it's a very full skirt…* that thought, too, came and went as Adjdaak spoke some unfamiliar words in his language and launched us into a swirling chaos. I had barely time to wonder about breathing before he touched down again outside an apartment building. Reverting to human form, he grasped my hand and we ran inside. I followed his lead: up one flight of stairs, down a hall, to rattle the knob of a locked door. Adjdaak knocked a hole in the door with one blow of his fist, kicked the splintered section below out with his bare foot, and dragged me into the apartment.

The first thing I saw was Rukshana, on the floor, gagged, in tears, and without her jeans.

The next thing was a face I'd have been happy never to see again: Craig, my jerk of an ex-boyfriend.

Laughing.

"Come to join the party?" he asked Adjdaak. "You're certainly dressed for it! But you didn't need to break the door down. I'd have been happy to let you in; no reason we can't both have a good time here."

Adjdaak growled as I fell to the floor beside Rukshana, feeling for the knots in the scarf that had gagged her. I winced away from the man and the dragon, expecting a blast of flame to engulf Craig.

Instead, Adjdaak turned around and *fled*.

I couldn't believe it. He was a *dragon* – and even in his human form, he could have beaten Craig to a pulp. Why this betrayal? Why now?

To hell with wondering – it was up to me, it seemed, to get Rukshana out of here. While she scrambled into her jeans I reached for some weapon, found nothing, stood up in front of her and snarled at Craig that we were going now.

He was staring at my face. "My God, what happened to you? I'm glad I got rid of you. You're way too ugly to fuck now. You can just take yourself off again, I'd rather have your little friend here." He swung at me; I dodged. He grabbed my arm and threw me back against the wall, head first. Dizzy, I slid partway to the floor, staggered upright again and prepared to launch myself at him.

"You're not going to hurt her! Rukshana, *run!*"

Before she got to her feet another man came through the broken door. Another rapist coming to the party? No – a boy, dressed in Taklan loose pants and overshirt, rubbing the sleep out of his eyes. He saw Rukshana, saw Craig reaching for her and threw himself on Craig.

"*Rustam!*" Rukshana cried out.

It was a totally unequal match, but the boy's fury seemed to give him strength. He pounded Craig with his fists while Craig tried to push him away; then a lucky blow sent Craig staggering back, eyes rolling up. As he slumped against the wall, Rustam pulled Rukshana upright.

"Oh... Rustam!" she said again. Her eyes were shining.

"Come on, get out of here!" he said in Taklan. He pushed her ahead of him through the shattered door. I followed them. Felt the back of my skirt being yanked back, heard the fabric tearing, threw myself into the hall, picked myself up and ran after the other two.

Adjdaak was out front. In dragon form again. All three of us scrambled onto his back and he said, *"B#z vlaad udjy Shaimak'd."*

Chaos again, and biting cold; a hard landing in darkness, and a roar that made the ground tremble. The kids fell off the dragon's back and Rustam took Rukshana's hand again.

"The boy saved your daughter," Adjdaak said in Taklan to two of the people who'd come running out of the houses. "He is a man now. And she is his woman." He switched to English. "Hold on, Sienna! *B#z vlaad udjy Taksus'd.*"

The cold surrounded me again and I grabbed for Adjdaak's neck spine. The village seemed to melt around me; shape and mass lost all meaning; I gasped in thin air, felt warmth, was in my own back yard.

Jenn was in her yard too, staring over the fence. Oh well – explanations later. I waved at her, hopped off Adjdaak, and ran into the house. A moment later he changed to human form and followed me, but this time he did stop in the laundry room to put his pants on.

And a good thing, too, because Michael was in the kitchen, staring at us as though we'd just popped out of nowhere. Which we had, I guess, and right in front of Jenn, but he couldn't have seen that.

"Where have you been?" he demanded.

"What was all that about?" I asked Adjdaak.

"It was better for Rustam to be her rescuer. The families will now permit that they become *erxtin.*"

I thought that over. Briefly. "Let me get this clear. In order to further Rukshana's love life, and not necessarily in the best direction, you were okay leaving me to fight off Craig?"

"Who's Craig?" Michael demanded. "And what *about* Rukshana?"

We had to put him in the picture before I could get back to my problem with Adjdaak's high-handed decisions. It took a while; he got inordinately upset about the fact that I'd gone off to tackle Rukshana's abductor alone.

"But I *wasn't* alone," I protested. "I had Adjdaak for backup."

Michael snorted. "Right. You were with a member of an alien species that, as far as we can find out, has neither morals nor common sense."

"If you mean that we do not tie ourselves up in ethical knots as do you humans," Adjdaak said, "I consider that—what is that thing you are always saying, Michael?"

The thing Michael actually seemed likely to say wouldn't have done our relationship with Adjdaak any good at all, so I stepped in. "You mean 'a feature, not a bug,' like people always say about software? I don't think you quite understand the phrase, Adjdaak. What it really means is that there is something badly wrong with the product and the seller is trying to cover it up by pretending that's what he meant all the time."

"No wonder your language hurts my head," Adjdaak grumbled. "In *my* language it is not possible to say what you do not mean."

"What, you don't have sarcasm?" Seemed to me he had plenty of that when he was speaking human languages, even if I couldn't think of any examples right off.

"Getting back to the point," Michael said with strained patience, "Who *is* this Craig, why did he attack Rukshana, and why did Adjdaak desert you at a critical moment?"

"I'm not exactly clear on the last part myself," I confessed.

"Fine, start at the other end. Craig?"

"Craig Bellish. A total jerk."

"And he targeted Rukshana... why?"

I sagged in my chair. "Because she's a very pretty girl with no sense at all when it comes to American men? Because I've been lounging around in bed, feeling sorry for myself, and leaving her unsupervised?"

"The man knew Sienna," Adjdaak observed. "That was obvious from what he said to her."

I winced. I'd been comforting myself with the fact that no one had heard Craig's cruel speech except Rukshana, and she'd been too upset to take it in. What I'd *thought* was a fact. "You weren't even there!"

"I did not have to be there to continue listening," he said.

Oh, great. Just great. We were dealing with an amoral being that could fly, breathe fire, transport himself anywhere instantaneously... and now he turned out to be a super eavesdropper as well!

"What he said—" Adjdaak began, looking at Michael.

"Doesn't matter now!" I interrupted him, while kicking his shin under the table. I glanced at Michael's face. Then I fixed my gaze on the table top.

"All right. I *do* know who he is. He's this creep I made the mistake of dating last year."

And strong evidence that, just like I'd believed ever since the mistake of my sophomore year in college, I was incompetent as a judge of character.

"He wasn't that bad then," I defended myself against the dismayed silence. "And it wasn't like – I mean, we were never *close*. He was so good-looking I couldn't believe he was interested in me, and he kept coming over and asking me out, and he didn't like it when I made excuses, and... well, I thought maybe I'd like him better when I got to know him..."

I trailed off into silence. My whole face was flaming now, not just the burned place. I decided to skip the part about Floss and Blossom staging a mini-intervention and pointing out to me that it was really stupid to keep dating a man when I didn't even enjoy his company. Given Michael's not unjustified opinion of the twins' collective IQ, he would hardly respect me more if I confessed they'd been smarter than I was about this relationship.

Not that it mattered, I thought drearily, because he wouldn't respect me anyway now that I'd confessed to getting mixed up with a man who turned out to enjoy raping young girls.

"I did break up with him, though," I said into a silence as thick as the clouds just before a thunderstorm. "He wasn't happy about it – he left angry. But he did leave, on his own. I mean, I didn't have to bring out my gun or anything. Honestly, I never guessed he could be violent! And I hadn't seen him since the day I told him to get out of my life."

"I wonder, though," Michael said quietly, "if he had seen *you*. Especially since we opened the business, you haven't exactly been keeping a low profile. Maybe he was still angry about being dumped."

It hadn't occurred to me in all these months, but Michael could be right. Certainly Craig had been furious at the time. And he was probably accustomed to getting what he wanted on the basis of his good looks. It was possible that nobody had ever turned him down so bluntly before. I nodded without looking up.

"Discovering that you were the fa- the head of a wildly successful business could have revived his anger."

He didn't need to avoid saying "face" around me. I didn't think. I was going to have to get used to it, wasn't I?

"Maybe he started off with the idea of stalking you. But you haven't been visible for several days."

And it would have been considerably longer, if I'd had my choice.

"And there was Rukshana in the front office. Beautiful, naïve, unsupervised, and it wouldn't have taken much effort to learn that you were treating her like a foster daughter. So he decided to hurt you through Rukshana."

I nodded again. It was all my fault, wasn't it? I'd let Craig into my life in the first place, I'd forgotten all about his temper tantrum when I broke up with him, I'd put Rukshana out front and hadn't paid nearly enough attention to her, even before I got hurt. Now, when it was too late, I wondered about those days when she'd supposedly stayed home to watch TV while I went to work. The thing with Craig could well have started before the home invasion, when I was perfectly well and strong and just didn't bother to keep tabs on Rukshana.

"Oh, Sienna," Michael sighed. "Don't look like that!"

"Like what?" I mumbled.

"Like you were carrying the whole world on your shoulders... and dropped it."

"I certainly dropped the ball."

"So did Adjdaak. So did I. So did Laura. We all knew that Rukshana was a crazy teenager, not an adult, and we all ignored her when she wasn't being an obvious problem."

"She wasn't your responsibility."

"If it comes to that," Michael told me, "she wasn't yours either. *Adjdaak* is the one who brought her into a world she couldn't understand. He should have been watching over her."

"This world is strange to me too," Adjdaak said, "and *she* asked *me* to bring her here. In Shaimak she would be counted as nearly adult. Did she become a child just because we were in America?"

Self-defense. Was it the beginning of a sense of right and wrong? Not that it really mattered; I hardly cared about the dragon's psychological development. I just wished he would go home to Taklanistan, where he belonged. I wished everybody would go away and leave me to my guilt and self-pity.

Now that Adjdaak had started explaining himself, the whole sequence of actions began to make more sense. He'd seen the attack on Rukshana as a chance to let the boy she loved, young Rustam, become a hero. It had been the work of seconds to speak himself back in Shaimak, to waken Rustam and bring him back to the apartment. He knew that Rukshana's parents had opposed her betrothal to Rustam not only because she was so young, but because they thought Rustam was too young and too shy to take on the duties of a husband. Now that he had saved Rukshana and brought her home, they would see things differently.

"And that's what you thought best for her? To marry at *fifteen*?"

"They will not marry at once. They will only become *erxtin*."

"I hope to God you mean that in a non-carnal sense!"

Adjdaak chose not to answer that directly. "Tell me, was Rukshana ever truly happy and at ease here?"

Pictures flashed through my mind. Rukshana buckling a pair of my jeans around her waist and saying that they were not too big, she needed pants that were loose enough to move around in. Rukshana kicking off the shoes I'd bought her as soon as we were at the office, because she was used to going barefoot indoors. Rukshana sleeping on the floor of the front room, wrapped in an old quilt, because American beds were too high and too soft and the covers were too warm.

Rukshana staring blankly at the Angry Birds app on my phone and asking if Americans were really so stupid that they couldn't tell the difference between these colored pictures and real birds that would steal the grain out of the fields.

"She liked pizza," I said, realizing how lame it sounded. "And ice cream."

Adjdaak snorted. "Both easy enough to export. After she marries and has a few babies, I would not be surprised if Rukshana starts the first pizza parlor in the Pamir Mountains."

Neither would I.

23. Dragonesse oblige

The most difficult part of the aftermath to Rukshana's adventure was persuading Michael not to pay a personal visit to Craig's apartment and finish the beating Rustam had started. The second most difficult part was persuading him not to call the cops. At least, those were the hard parts that involved somebody else.

"Either way," I said, "whether you beat him up yourself or call the cops, the police *will* get involved and they *will* have questions we don't want to answer. Where's the victim? 'Oh, she was never legally here, and now she's back home in Central Asia.' How did she get here in the first place? 'A dragon brought her.' What did you use to splinter Craig's apartment door? 'Oh, our friend the dragon did that while he was in human form. Barefoot.'"

Michael subsided, but he did mutter about dark alleys and strictly off-the-record retribution. And I didn't discourage him. He was frustrated enough about not being able to find the Russians who'd put me in the hospital. It was fine with me if he did anything to Craig short of murder, just as long as he didn't get caught and give the cops a clue they could follow all the way back to my unofficial guests. And pretty soon, with any luck, I'd be all out of guests. Now that Rukshana was back home, Adjdaak didn't really need to stick around, did he?

The really difficult part, of course, was that now I had plenty of time to remember what Craig had said when he saw my face. After Adjdaak went outside to imitate a rock garden, I stayed in the kitchen, moodily twisting my skirt around to complete the work of destruction Craig had started when he grabbed the bottom flounce.

"Sienna." Michael looked worried. Why? From his perspective everything had ended well. "What's the matter? You look totally crushed. Did that son of a bitch do anything to you that you didn't tell me?"

Not with his hands.

"I guess I'm just shaken up by the whole experience." I pulled another length of fabric loose. "Don't worry… Look at this. It's a good thing this skirt had a lace insertion above the bottom flounce; when Craig tore it, he didn't do anything I can't fix by pulling the whole flounce free and stitching it back just above the lace."

"Sienna, you don't even own a sewing machine."

"Jenn has one." Actually, she had three machines: a regular sewing machine, a serger, and a thing that punched barbed needles through fabric to do something with merino fibers. "I'm sure she won't mind if I go over to use it for an hour or so."

"Mmm. In that case, why don't you cut off everything that got torn, and put a new band of lace above the flounce. A wider one," he suggested. "Or maybe you could substitute lace for the whole flounce. I like the peekaboo effect. Did I ever tell you what great legs you have?"

Maybe if he focused on the legs, he wouldn't be so put off by my marred face. For a while, anyway. Eventually he would look at me and realize that…

I wiped my eyes with the strip of fabric that I'd ripped free.

"*Sienna.*" Michael dragged his chair next to mine and put his arms around me. "Tell me."

A lady, my aunts had insisted, might allow a few tears to fall from time to time, but she never forgot herself to the point where her face got red and swollen and her nose got stuffed up. Well, fine. I wasn't a lady, and my face was already past praying for. I blew my nose on the loose fabric strip.

"When Craig saw what happened to my face…"

"What, did he pretend to care about you?"

"Quite the reverse. And he d-didn't say anything that wasn't true. He just said that he was g-glad he g-got rid of me, because now I was too ugly to…" My throat closed up.

"What do you mean, he didn't say anything that wasn't true," Michael demanded. "He didn't get rid of you – you dumped him. You just told me so. And you don't lie." His arm tightened around my shoulders, and with his free hand he turned my tear-swollen face up to meet his. "And the rest of it was lies too. You're *not* ugly. You're brave and beautiful and if that wound does scar, which it won't, you'll wear it as a badge of honor."

"I'd rather be pretty than have a 'badge of honor' that everybody shrinks from."

"They won't."

"How do you know? What if it never fades? Eventually you'll get tired of having people point and whisper whenever we go out. You'll get tired of l-looking at me."

Michael kissed me. "Sienna. I didn't fall in love with your face. I fell in love with a lady whose eyes blazed like a tiger's when she was angry, a lady who faced me down with her father's gun when she was so scared that even her freckles turned green."

I managed a chuckle. "I don't think you felt all that romantic when I was pointing the gun at you."

"You'd be surprised. Okay, the thought of a stray bullet ripping through my flesh *was* kind of a turnoff... but afterwards... You'd be surprised how many fantasies that scene inspired."

"Like what?"

"Oh... too kinky to tell you right now, but maybe I'll demonstrate some time." He paused. "Without, of course, the actual gun, because I don't approve of playing with real guns. Think I could find a black water pistol at Toy Joy to use as a prop?"

I laughed then, and even started believing that things could work out all right.

And for a while that seemed to be true. My black eye faded, and the burn on my face healed to the point that I didn't have to wear a dressing over it to protect the raw skin. I kept an eye out for Jenn while I was home just reading and puttering around; for the first couple of days after I got out of the hospital I had been too wrapped up in my own self-pity to thank her properly. Now, for some reason, we never seemed to run into each other. She didn't even come over to ask why I hadn't planted the seedlings she'd given me. Maybe she was busy making dolls.

I went back to work on the Monday after the home invasion. A few people – well, to be precise, all of the male tutors who came in – wanted to know where Rukshana was. Fortunately I was able to answer that without even lying.

"She was only visiting me for a short while. She's gone back to her parents now."

"Ah, end of spring break in their public school system. She'd have to be getting back to school, I suppose," said one of them.

Always helps if you let people tell you what they'd like to believe.

My week's absence had, fortunately, coincided with UT's spring break, and Gabriela Gehrig had worked wonders by way of rescheduling the few clients of mine who had stayed in town over the vacation. Those happened to be the ones who were most desperate to get their reading proficiency tests out of the way, so they'd made no complaints about substitute tutors.

"They did seem to be more satisfied when it was you tutoring them," Gabriela said.

Yes! The Sienna System worked far better than random tutors could!

"I suppose some people are never happy unless they're getting personal attention from the boss," she added with a sniff.

And sometimes people tell you what you would *not* like to believe. I tamped down my springing enthusiasm and looked over the rest of what had happened in my absence. Gabriela had a healthy list of would-be tutors for me to interview; if even half of them worked out, we'd have the major European languages covered with no more need for me to run around from tutorial to tutorial like a chicken with my head cut off.

Michael had returned the scheduling system to something like what it had been before I overrode it, only now the constraints on me were even greater: no more than three tutorial sessions in any one day, and no more than twelve sessions in a week. Ouch. The part of the business I liked best was the one-on-one interaction with students. Okay, I'd learned that I couldn't just do that and manage the business in my nonexistent spare time. But would it really take all the hours that this new schedule freed up? Michael was supposed to be the business manager as well as IT expert, shouldn't he be doing some of whatever management issues cropped up?

"Oh, I'll have plenty to do," Michael said when I raised that point with him. "You're forgetting that you need to drop in on all the other tutors regularly, to help them get used to working your way. If they all just play it by ear, the way they would have when working independently –"

"Oh, okay, I get it, I get it." My original vision for Sienna Language Services had, though I hadn't realized it, required me to work the equivalent of three full-time jobs. Michael had done a brilliant job in cutting that down to a job and a half; now it was time for me to do my part. The life of an Austin slacker was still receding into my past. Oh well, at least as a supervising tutor I'd still be working with individuals, so that part would be almost as satisfying as doing the tutoring myself.

It was also going to require me to show my face to every single tutor who was working for us, as well as to all the new contractors Gabriela had lined up for interviews. That part made me more nervous than anything else, even though getting through this first day back at work should have dispelled some of the nervousness. I'd applied Floss and Blossom's magic healing/concealing ointment to both the burn and the fading bruises around my eye before coming in to work, refreshed it in the bathroom in mid-morning, and applied a whole new coat after lunch. There'd been a few curious glances but only a couple of tentative questions along the lines of, "Did those guys who broke into your house hurt you?" to which I responded, "No biggie, it'll heal in a couple of weeks, and where are your notes on that Tamil tutoring session with the anthropology major?"

Certainly nobody had been so crass as to exclaim, "My God, woman, what happened to your face?"

"Told you so," said Floss when she and Blossom dropped by that evening to hear how my first day back in public had gone.

"It's really good concealer," Blossom said. "Now wash your face so I can put on some clear Vitamin E ointment. Floss –"

"On it," Floss said, backing out of the living room with the plastic bag she'd brought in. A few minutes later I heard the subdued roar of the blender, and then Floss came back carrying a tumbler of some evil-looking, murky green liquid.

"Do I put that on before or after the Vitamin E stuff?" I inquired.

"Neither," Blossom said. "You drink it. It's a kale, blueberry and papaya smoothie. Loaded with antioxidants and vitamins. I bet you had junk for lunch."

"A tuna sandwich."

"On white bread?"

"Natch."

"From now on, if you must eat bread, pick whole grains." Blossom frowned. "Maybe I ought to pack a lunch for you every day."

I shuddered at the thought, envisioning a healthy spinach-kale salad with who knew what antioxidant miracle foods concealed under the leaves. "Uh, I don't want to take up so much of your time. I promise I'll be good." And to prove it, I drained the smoothie. It wasn't quite as bad as it looked, but it sure wasn't anything I'd drink on purpose.

"Next time I'll put in strawberries too," Floss promised.

That would certainly be an improvement, but it didn't fix the simple fact that stuff you drink should not be *green*. I don't even care for the green beer that some misguided people serve on St. Patrick's day, much less for thick green drinks based on veggies.

I got the spinach-kale salad anyway. For dinner. It was packed with sunflower seeds and avocado slices and walnuts, all of which I picked out and enjoyed in between dutifully chewing the leafy stuff.

Michael and Laura went out for dinner and came back bearing a bag of pot roast and chuck steaks for Adjdaak. I eyed the raw meat enviously and mentioned that I was still hungry.

"Brought you something too," said Michael.

A hamburger?

"Better eat it before it melts."

Not a hamburger.

He brought out a smaller plastic bag and flourished a pint of dark chocolate fudge ripple toffee ice cream. "I did my research. Did you know dark chocolate is full of antioxidants?"

"Please tell Floss and Blossom," I begged while he located a spoon. I dug into the ice cream, clutching the carton in case anybody else thought they were getting any before I was sated. "If they keep standing over me while I eat healthy stuff, I'm going to turn into a rabbit. A *hungry* rabbit," I emphasized before digging out a lovely piece of crunchy chocolate-covered toffee.

The first day back at work might have started off kind of tense, but it couldn't have ended better. Who'd have thought that Michael, the man who thought it was adventurous to order strawberry ice cream instead of vanilla, would plunge into the wonderland of Amy's special flavor mixes just for me?

And later that night, he demonstrated in most convincing style that he wasn't put off one bit by the burn mark running up my cheek.

During the rest of that week it seemed that everybody was happy. The magic concealing foundation did its trick so well that I didn't even think about the mark except when I washed my face. Jenn kept bringing over herbal poultices for me to apply after work, and Floss and Blossom eased up and allowed some things I could taste and chew into those blasted kale salads. Laura's new song was such a hit that she spent the evenings performing and the days working out an accompaniment for the band to play. And Michael, after supposedly spending a night at his own place while Adjdaak stood guard here, turned up for breakfast the next morning with scraped knuckles, a bruise on the side of his jaw, and a look of blissful satisfaction that made me think he was no longer carrying a grudge against Craig.

"Did you put him in the hospital?" I whispered when Laura was busy with the dishes.

He looked regretful. "You didn't want me to do anything that would interest the police. He could have been hurt in a bar fight, that's what I recommended he tell people unless he really wanted to say he'd been beaten up by somebody three inches shorter and five years older. Let's just say he will be strongly motivated to stay the hell away from you in the future."

I guess I'm not ever going to be the nice lady my aunts tried to raise, because I was totally delighted with this conclusion to *l'affaire Craig*.

The only remaining problem was Adjdaak, and he had more or less promised to go away. In his own time – after Dragonfest. It would be rude, he said, to disappear just before his own personal festival and to disappoint his worshippers. *Dragonesse oblige*, he said.

I'd never noticed Adjdaak being so punctilious about politeness before. In general, he seemed to regard it as one of those meaningless human customs like wearing pants. I suspected his decision had more to do with vanity. In Shaimak he never got to appear before an audience of thousands, their belief fueled by copious amounts of beer. Oh, well – so he wanted to overfly the park once or twice before heading home to be a father figure to his hatchlings. What harm could it do?

24. A shower of sparks

Dragonfest, like the opening of Sienna Language Services, had been scheduled under pressure. Two weeks wasn't much time to create an open-air festival. But Eeyore's Birthday Party was happening less than a month later, and then there would be Cinco de Mayo, and from then until the end of the school year there would be an unending stream of lesser events to take advantage of the balmy weather. People who wanted to cash in on, I mean celebrate, the rumors of a dragon in Austin had to get their act together quickly.

The organizers were lucky. Early April in Austin can bring spring showers or a reprise of chilly winter days, but this weekend was sunny and just warm enough to interest attendees in the beer kegs and Sno-Cone stands dotted around the park. Costumers had done a brisk business in the fancy wear they mostly rented out only for Renaissance Faires, face painters had come out of the bushes, and the enterprising vendor who was selling dragon kites sold out long before Michael and I had even ambled over to take in the sights. Laura, of course, couldn't come with us; today she was one of the attractions. In a dress that looked as if it was made of overlapping dragon scales, green at the top and flame-colored at the hem, she was scheduled for three appearances at the bandstand to sing the hit song that had become the unofficial anthem of Dragonfest.

As long as Adjdaak stuck to the plan, I thought he should be able to make his appearance and get home afterwards safely enough. We had had lengthy discussions about what I thought of as cosmetics and Michael considered costuming. Although Adjdaak initially considered it ridiculous to suggest that he needed any costume to add splendor to his naturally splendid body, he had come around to our suggestions in the end. He even understood that the impact would be greatest if he did not make his appearance until sunset. A couple of hours after sunset would have been even better in my opinion, but some idiot had mentioned that at this time of year, the audience for outdoor events tended to disperse rapidly once it got dark. That was the price we'd paid for letting Duke in on the planning; Adjdaak flatly refused to risk "disappointing" his worshippers by waiting to appear until some of them had given up and gone home.

As I hoped, after this, he himself would do.

Michael and I spread out an old blanket and sat down to enjoy the refreshments (Shiner Prickly Pear beer for him, raspberry shaved ice for me) while the band warmed the audience up for Laura's third and final appearance. Two little boys whose faces had been artistically transformed into snarling dragon masks ran around us for a while, flapping the pointy cloaks that were being sold as "dragon wings" and asking why we couldn't just sit on the grass.

"'Cause we're old," Michael said equably. "Our poor old bones can't take sitting on the damp ground for hours. D'you want Gramma and me to be crippled with rheumatism?"

"I think you're lying," one of the kids said.

The other one pointed at my face. "What happened to you?"

My hand went up automatically to cover the healing scar, but Michael trapped it under his while I was counting to three in Turkish. "Dragon encounter," he said. "Gramma is a very, very brave lady."

The band switched from one of Duke's atonal-alternative compositions to a polka – nobody could say they weren't eclectic – and the boys ran off to improvise their own hopping, bobbing dance to the music.

This would be the third and final session, timed so that Laura would be singing as the sun sank and the sky darkened, with lights on her shimmering dress to make it look as though she were clothed in scales and flames. And the close of her song was supposed to be Adjdaak's cue to make a *very brief* appearance. I hoped. Acting on somebody else's cue was not exactly one of the dragon's strong points.

***

Lying in the small clump of bushes, Zhenya sweated and wished Bogdan were holding the missile launcher instead of him. He would have *happily* ceded his place in the bushes and his chance of fame back home to Bogdan. He would have been more than willing to stay back at the motel, in fact. But no, Bogdan insisted on having him there, just because Bogdan's burns covered both his shoulders and made it hard to heft the missile launcher. Zhenya had burns too, didn't he? And why did every kind of plant that grew in the *oblast* of Texas hate people? He had one kind of rash on his hands and another creeping up his ankles and he'd been there long enough to fill up his pee bottle and there was absolutely no sign that the dragon was going to show itself today. Why should it? The park below his observation post had beer, cotton candy, cones of shaved ice, face painters, costume and puppet vendors – in short, it was a disgusting display of greedy capitalist excess – but it was totally lacking in vodka and tethered goats. Unless this dragon had gone rogue and started eating humans, what was there to attract it here?

Zhenya sighed and quit scanning the horizon for a while to watch the people prancing around the park with their balloons and beer mugs. Some of the costumes were indeed quite innovative; he was particularly taken by the twin blonde girls wearing jeweled bikini tops and long transparent harem pants and carrying signs declaring themselves to be Certified Virgin Dragon Bait. If his burns didn't still hurt so much, he could've volunteered to check their certifications.

***

"Do you suppose Blossom and Floss have ever heard of truth in advertising?" I asked idly as they pranced past our little corner for the third time.

"Oh, I'm sure they found somebody to certify them," Michael said. "Besides, Adjdaak says he doesn't really insist on virgins."

"He's not *supposed* to eat humans at all. Rukshana said he promised after that distressing episode with the revolutionary terrorists."

"Too bad. I'd happily feed him those Russian bastards who hurt you, if they hadn't disappeared."

You'd have thought two men suffering from severe burns would have been easy enough to find in Austin, but nobody like that had turned up at any of the hospitals and emergency rooms. And I suspected the cops hadn't put a lot of energy into the search. I'd been pretty woozy when they first interviewed me, and the only explanation I could come up with for the men being on fire was that they'd been careless around the open flames of the gas burner. It wasn't like I could admit to having set them on fire with a language that didn't exist, using magic that didn't exist, spoken by beings who also didn't exist.

The music was rising as Laura approached the end of her song.

"My love is the dragon, my love is the fire…"

Fire was not my favorite subject these days. I winced, trying not to remember, and missed the line about her heart's desire.

"He is my home!"

The applause crashed over the last chords like rising waves. Laura bowed, the lights went down, and… the whole park was darker. Something rode the western clouds, cutting off the light from the setting sun.

There were shrieks now. People pointed. The screams were louder than the clapping, and half the people in the park were trying to run, only there was nowhere to run to and they were impeded by the other half, who were standing with their arms raised, waving to and welcoming the dragon their belief had called into existence. Or something like that. I mean, I'm pretty sure they didn't realize they were waving to a dragon who'd casually dropped in from Taklanistan for a couple of cheeseburgers and a large pizza or two.

As a dark silhouette against the evening sky, Adjdaak was breathtaking. The span of his wings seemed to overshadow the entire park, and the undulations of his faintly glowing blue-black scales filled the sky overhead.

Then, just as the sun dipped below the western hills, his sinuous neck bent and he breathed fire – not over his worshippers, but over the lines of fuse cord that Michael and I had carefully trailed along his scales so that he'd be able to reach them with one gout of flame.

For a moment his flanks and stomach were lighted by the flickering lines of fire. Then the fireworks caught.

Sparklers lashed to the points of his wings blazed out in glowing spheres of sparks; golden lines of fire ran in to his shoulders and back out again; each clawed foot grasped a flaming Catherine wheel. He was a veritable light show of a dragon.

"You don't suppose they'll hurt him, do you?" I asked Michael under the roar of the crowd.

"Not a chance. He wouldn't have let us attach the fireworks if there were any danger."

I tried to share Michael's faith in the dragon's good sense. Truth to tell, I wasn't quite that convinced of it. Adjdaak's people had the reputation of valuing glory above safety. Still, he *was* a creature of earth and fire. A few little human-made fireworks couldn't hurt a being whose own body generated enough flame to roast a goat... could they?

Then there was a burst of light, *not* from Adjdaak, and a deafening crash. Above me I heard a roar of fury, and flames stabbed out of Adjdaak's opened jaws to catch the figures of two men standing among bushes, on the little ridge above the park.

I don't remember exactly how things happened next, I mean in what order. The men Adjdaak had lanced his flames at screamed, I'm pretty sure of that, but the screams were short-lived. After a horrified pause, I think the closest festival goers ran to help them. But I thought it would be too late... and by that time Adjdaak had disappeared.

"Home," Michael said, ruthlessly towing me through the crowd and back to where we'd parked.

"Adjdaak?"

"Not here. I'm hoping he sent himself to your back yard. Otherwise... Do you think he could have gone as far as Taklanistan?"

"Why not?"

Michael opened the car door for me, waited to make sure I fastened the seat belt, then came around to the other side.

"Because," he said, starting the car and zipping around two larger cars that I'd thought were blocking our exit, "I've heard weapons that make that kind of noise, and I think he might be hurt."

I thought that over in between the brief, wordless prayers that I sent up while Michael exercised his military-grade driving skills to get us out of the park ahead of everybody else who was trying to leave. "They shot at him before. With rifles. All that happened was, he lost a few scales."

"Yes, well, this wasn't a rifle," Michael said, breaking the speed limit and a few minor traffic laws. "Told you, I know that sound. Some bastard got hold of a shoulder-mounted anti-tank missile launcher."

I held onto the edge of the seat with both hands as he made a hard left that wasn't *quite* running a red light. I hoped the traffic cameras would see it the same way.

"Isn't that illegal?"

"Very," Michael said. "But so is breaking into houses and tying up women and—"

I made a small sound and he stopped abruptly. "Sorry. Point is, I don't think these s.o.b.'s had any limits. And even Adjdaak may not be immune to heavy-duty artillery."

He screeched to a stop in front of my house and we both jumped out while the car was still shaking. I didn't waste time unlocking the front door; the fastest way to the back yard was around the side, through the unlocked gate in the fence.

25. Magic where you least expect it

He had crashed down awkwardly, head on the back steps, body sprawled out with the tail flopping over the fence into Jenn's yard. He was lying on his side, breathing rapidly and shallowly; the faintly luminescent scales shook with the irregular pattern of his ragged breaths. He opened one eye as I ran to his head. The glowing topaz was dimmed, patterns like grey smoke swirling across it.

"Adjdaak... *Adjdaak!*"

He gave a great, belching, smoky sigh.

"What happened to you?" I demanded.

"I told you," Michael said behind me. "Anti-tank missile."

"Is that what you call it?" Adjdaak rumbled. "What is a tank?"

"Apparently," Michael said, "it is also an anti-dragon missile." He knelt by Adjdaak's raised foreleg and clicked on the tiny super-flashlight he kept attached to his key fob. The circle of harsh blue light wavered over Adjdaak's exposed underside and steadied on an ugly gaping hole with edges like raw meat. Half a dozen scales had fallen on the ground beneath the wound, and others were hanging by a thread; when Adjdaak coughed, two more scales fell off. "No external bleeding," Michael said as if to himself.

"I can... slow my blood loss..." Adjdaak said. He sounded sleepy, and I thought the blue edges of his scales were dimming. "But I feel... as if I had swallowed a poisoned goat. Without chewing."

I clutched Michael's arm. "What does that mean? Can you help him?" Oh, I wished Rukshana were here. She might have known enough about dragon anatomy to be useful.

"Bring me a skewer from the kitchen. And rubbing alcohol."

And to think I'd planned to throw out that skewer set because of its nightmare associations!

Adjdaak clearly did not enjoy having the wound probed after Michael sterilized the skewer. I gave him props for not accidentally flaming my boyfriend. I gave Michael more props for taking that chance.

Couldn't I do anything more useful than standing around admiring the men?

"Adjdaak," Michael asked, frowning, "are your people particularly susceptible to radioactive substances?"

"What are those?"

"You know, like U-238?"

Adjdaak groaned. "I am in no condition to play word games."

"And we don't have time for the short course in radiation poisoning, so I'm going to take that as a yes." Michael turned to me. "The missile didn't penetrate deeply, it barely got through his scales. I don't *think* it could have damaged any vital organs. And he's stopped any potential blood loss. The only thing I can think of is, a lot of anti-tank munitions use depleted uranium."

"Eew. You guys in the Army go around giving people radiation poisoning?"

"*Depleted*," Michael emphasized. "Apart from a few tinfoil-hat types, nobody thinks one of these shells is going to spatter deadly radiation across the target. It's the big hole it punches that'll kill you, not the slight radioactive aftermath. But the big hole didn't kill Adjdaak, did it? With his control over blood flow, he shouldn't be in any immediate danger. Unless there's some factor that puts him at more risk than us. Like being super-sensitive to trace amounts of radiation."

"Wouldn't that have made him sick already? I mean, there's radon in the soil…" Real estate agents, trust me, know *all* about radon and how much people can get upset over a teeny trickle of totally natural background radiation.

"But that's not actually in his body," Michael pointed out. "Quite likely the scales perform a secondary function of shielding him from radiation in the environment."

"Pray do not allow my imminent death to disturb your academic discussion," Adjdaak said, rolling the eye we could see.

The glowing topaz of his eye was definitely dimmer smokier than it had been a few minutes ago. And when Michael turned off the flashlight for a moment, I could see that the edges of Adjdaak's scales were fading.

"We'll have to get it out," Michael decided. "Right away! I need a pair of forceps."

I stared at him. "Forceps? I'm not a medical supply store. How about the kitchen tongs?"

"Too big. I'm afraid they'd do more damage to his structure. Come on, Sienna. You've got all that girly stuff. Tweezers –"

"*Way* too small."

"Nail files—"

"You want to excavate his wound with another sharp pointy thing?"

"There must be *something*."

And by then I had, actually thought of something. The only catch was that it wasn't in my house.

It would be at Jenn's.

At first I thought Jenn wasn't going to answer her door. Was she even in town? I hadn't actually seen her since... Oh.

I hadn't seen her since she'd seen *me*, popping into the back yard out of thin air after Adjdaak had rescued Rukshana and taken her back to her home.

That would be *Adjdaak* and me, actually. He would definitely have been the star exhibit in that little episode.

And what had I done to reassure Jenn? Not a damn thing. We'd run inside and found Michael, and I had been all about figuring out just what had been going on with Adjdaak and Rukshana and that bastard Craig, and I'd never even tried to explain what was happening to my nosy neighbor. Not that I had any idea what I would have said, but leaving her to wonder if she was going crazy or what... Yep, I'd definitely dropped the ball there. No wonder I hadn't noticed her around lately! I was probably the last person in the world she wanted to have any contact with.

And that was just too damn bad, because if I didn't get hold of the tools we needed, and fast, Adjdaak was not going to make it. There was a light on at the back of Jenn's house. I pounded on the door and yelled, "Jenn! Jenn! I need your help!"

She was white and shaking when she finally got to the door, but she let me in.

"Is this about that dragon?" she demanded.

"Uh. I, ah, I guess you noticed us the other day?"

"I did," Jenn said, "and I've been trying to decide what I believe about that. It has not been easy." She gave a shaky laugh. "Goodness knows, I of all people *ought* to be able to understand."

That didn't make any sense to me, but it also didn't seem to be important. What mattered was that Jenn didn't waste any time playing I-don't-believe-you games when I told her that Adjdaak was badly hurt and I needed her tools, even though I'd forgotten the word and said, 'those long skinny metal things that you grab with to turn tubes inside out.'"

"Hemostats," Jenn said, turning to the sewing niche that took up half her living room. She picked up some shiny metal clamps and dropped them in a tote bag. "Needles? Sutures?" A big curving needle, a pair of pliers, a spool of white thread went into the bag. "Go back, start boiling some water to sterilize these. I'll be there after I pack a few more supplies."

"Michael used rubbing alcohol…"

"We're going to do this *right*," Jenn said crisply.

I raced back to the kitchen. Bless Michael – he already had the spaghetti pot full of bubbling water. "We'll need light," Jenn said after a glance at Adjdaak under the dim illumination of the back porch bulb. "Michael, I left the house unlocked. There's a closet where I keep the lights for photo shoots." She gave him directions and he headed over there at a run. While Jenn sterilized her doll-making tools and a loose skein of fine silk thread, he set up the lights on their own stands, one on either side of Adjdaak's torn belly.

"Hold his head," she told me while she pulled on latex gloves. "Distract him. You help her!" she told Michael. "I've got this."

Michael mentioned his field medic training and Jenn shook her head. "You're the strongest of us. I need you to help Sienna hold his head; I don't want him accidentally incinerating me while I work. This might pinch just a little bit," she told Adjdaak before taking out the sterilized hemostat.

While Michael rested his hands on Adjdaak's jaw and blocked his view of the proceedings, and my neighbor knelt in front of the wound and probed ever so delicately with her longest hemostat, I sat on my own back porch with a dragon's head on my lap, asking him to explain the system of position markers in his language. What? What would *you* talk about to a wounded dragon? It worked, didn't it? While Adjdaak somewhat snappishly corrected my misunderstandings – the particles for place were suffixes but those for origin were prefixes, as should be obvious to the meanest intelligence – Jenn found the depleted uranium missile, extracted it, and stitched Adjdaak's wound shut with white silk threaded through that nasty-looking curving needle. The pliers, it turned out, were for pulling that needle through the edges of the belly scales on each side of the wound.

"Okay, big boy," she said, patting his side. "All done now, and *weren't* you a big, brave boy?"

Adjdaak stretched out his neck to lay his head in her lap. Both topaz eyes rolled up and he gave a contented grunt. His tongue lolled out of his jaws and he looked almost like a very big, very relaxed hound.

"Jenn, I – I can't begin to thank you," I started. "For this, and... for finding me the other day and treating my burn, and..."

Jenn waved her hand. "There's only one favor I want in return," she told me. Her eyes passed over Adjdaak's recumbent form and she gave a little sigh. "I can't believe how I convinced myself he was just a pile of rocks. I guess you aren't going to be planting those *scutellaria* seedlings, are you?"

"They wouldn't really have much of a chance to take root," I said. "Adjdaak will be going home as soon as he is well enough to travel."

Jenn blushed, cleared her throat. "Yes, well. About that favor..."

I collected the scales Adjdaak had lost to his wound, but he wasn't interested in them; he was already growing new scales to replace the loss. I put them away in the gun safe as mementos of the whole episode.

"You're not going to sell them?" Michael asked.

"To whom? Hank already has that one you got for him and he'll be perfectly happy with that as long as he thinks it's the only one in the Western world. And I certainly don't want to attract more Russian thugs. Besides, selling them would kind of destroy our story that there was never a dragon here in the first place." But I couldn't quite bring myself to throw them away. Some day I might need to remind myself that I'd been visited by a dragon.

The only remaining clues to Adjdaak's visit aren't a problem, because they masquerade as the product of Jenn's creative imagination. Her new line of dolls, the Back Yard Dragons, is selling extremely well. She took copious photos and made detailed drawings while Adjdaak was convalescing, and he has promised to bring his mate back for a visit some day so that she can get a good look at a female dragon. In return, she has promised me that one of the days she will introduce me to one of the "little friends" who were the live models for her Woodland Elves and Fern Fairies lines.

It seems that magic is everywhere, especially where you least expect it.

Also by Margaret Ball

Dragon speech series:

The Language of the Dragon *A nonhuman language allows a young linguist to warp reality… at the price of possible brain damage.*

Applied Topology series:

A Pocketful of Stars
A quiet math major has to fight in the magical realm for her life and those of her friends after the CIA decides to make use of her paranormal abilities.

An Opening in the Air
When a rival mage attacks, Thalia needs wits as well as magic to save the Center for Applied Topology. And the defense may cost her the man she loves.

An Annoyance of Grackles
It's bad enough when a rival mage tries to destroy you. When he turns out to be a god, that's worse. And when the god teams up with the most notorious contract bomber in America? If Thalia can't outwit the duo, she may wind up scattered across the campus in tiny pieces.

A Tapestry of Fire
Saving her best friend from life as a fish is difficult. Rescuing the man she loves from a past era of fire and fury ought to be impossible, so it may take Thalia a little longer.

A Creature of Smokeless Flame
When CIA officers' children are kidnapped for revenge, Thalia and her colleagues follow the trail across the continents to an African terrorists' camp whose leader has the help of his own personal genie.

A Revolution of Rubies
When Thalia started working directly for the CIA, she didn't expect to follow a trail of stolen rubies to a Central Asian country in the throes of revolution – much less to be taken hostage by the revolutionaries.

Regency Magic series:

Salt Magic
Sabira can deal with her underwater family and with mysterious murders and encroaching sea monsters on land. The hard part is explaining to the man whom she comes to love that she is not exactly human.

Harmony series:

Insurgents
Awakening
Survivors

Earlier books:

Disappearing Act
Duchess of Aquitaine
Mathemagics
Lost in Translation
No Earthly Sunne
Changeweaver
Flameweaver
The Shadow Gate

www.ingramcontent.com/pod-product-compliance
Lightning Source LLC
Chambersburg PA
CBHW022114170626
46808CB00002B/718